Naked Justice

At that moment all three of them heard something from the front of the house. Apparently, the flimsy shack had a good front door, and Virgil had been unable to force it without making some kind of noise.

The man's head jerked around. Clint saw his face, but didn't recognize him.

Through the window Clint heard a woman's voice.

The man didn't answer. He got off the bed and grabbed his gun, moved toward the bedroom door, which was also closed. If Virgil came through that door, he'd be dead before he knew it.

Clint smashed out the window, pointed his gun into the room, and said, "Hold it!"

The naked man turned his head toward the window, then brought the gun around. At that moment the bedroom door crashed open. The girl had screamed at the sound of breaking glass, and screamed again when the door slammed open.

Clint fired once. The bullet hit the man in the chest, driving him backward until the back of his legs hit the bed. He fell over on top of the girl, who kept right on screaming.

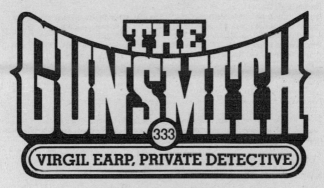

THE GUNSMITH

333

VIRGIL EARP, PRIVATE DETECTIVE

J. R. ROBERTS

JOVE BOOKS, NEW YORK

THE BERKLEY PUBLISHING GROUP
Published by the Penguin Group
Penguin Group (USA) Inc.
375 Hudson Street, New York, New York 10014, USA
Penguin Group (Canada), 90 Eglinton Avenue East, Suite 700, Toronto, Ontario M4P 2Y3, Canada
(a division of Pearson Penguin Canada Inc.)
Penguin Books Ltd., 80 Strand, London WC2R 0RL, England
Penguin Group Ireland, 25 St. Stephen's Green, Dublin 2, Ireland (a division of Penguin Books Ltd.)
Penguin Group (Australia), 250 Camberwell Road, Camberwell, Victoria 3124, Australia
(a division of Pearson Australia Group Pty. Ltd.)
Penguin Books India Pvt. Ltd., 11 Community Centre, Panchsheel Park, New Delhi—110 017, India
Penguin Group (NZ), 67 Apollo Drive, Rosedale, North Shore 0632, New Zealand
(a division of Pearson New Zealand Ltd.)
Penguin Books (South Africa) (Pty.) Ltd., 24 Sturdee Avenue, Rosebank, Johannesburg 2196,
South Africa

Penguin Books Ltd., Registered Offices: 80 Strand, London WC2R 0RL, England

This is a work of fiction. Names, characters, places, and incidents either are the product of the author's imagination or are used fictitiously, and any resemblance to actual persons, living or dead, business establishments, events, or locales is entirely coincidental.

VIRGIL EARP, PRIVATE DETECTIVE

A Jove Book / published by arrangement with the author

PRINTING HISTORY
Jove edition / September 2009

Copyright © 2009 by Robert J. Randisi.
Cover illustration by Sergio Giovine.

ISBN: 978-0-515-14694-3

JOVE®
Jove Books are published by The Berkley Publishing Group,
a division of Penguin Group (USA) Inc.,
375 Hudson Street, New York, New York 10014.
JOVE® is a registered trademark of Penguin Group (USA) Inc.
The "J" design is a trademark of Penguin Group (USA) Inc.

PRINTED IN THE UNITED STATES OF AMERICA

10   9   8   7   6   5   4   3   2   1

ONE

Colton, California, was a coming town, but it was also a town concerned with being as modern as possible. For this reason there were no bordellos, and liquor was only served in a few licensed saloons.

These were things Clint Adams didn't know yet as he rode into town. He had been in San Diego visiting his friend Wyatt Earp. Wyatt had told him that his brother Virgil had opened a detective agency in the northern California town of Colton. While Clint's association with the Earps always boiled down to his friendship with Wyatt, he'd decided to ride north and see how Virgil was doing in his new profession.

"James and Nick are also there," Wyatt told him, "although I'm not sure what they're doin' with themselves these days."

James was the youngest of the Earp brothers, while Nick was the Earp patriarch. More often than not, Nick Earp was a saloon owner. Clint assumed this was the profession he would find the older Earp plying in Colton.

As far as Clint could tell, none of the Earps had yet recovered from the murder of their brother Morgan in Tombstone, which had followed the whole O.K. Corral debacle. He knew that Wyatt blamed himself for Morgan's death, but he assumed that Virgil would also be shouldering some of that guilt, even though Virgil himself had been shot and crippled.

Clint reined Eclipse in as they reached a hotel and he decided to go inside and get a room before taking the big Darley Arabian to the livery stable.

The Hotel Colton, on Pennsylvania Street, was a new building and still smelled of fresh-cut wood. The lobby was spacious, well furnished, and the clerk behind the desk even seemed well scrubbed, his hair slicked down and parted in the middle.

"Good day to you, sir," he said in greeting.

"I'd like a room."

"Certainly, sir. We are happy to oblige. Please sign the register."

The clerk, in his forties, was way too enthusiastic for his age, as far as Clint was concerned. He turned to pluck a key from a rack behind him.

"And how long will you be staying with us, sir?" the clerk asked.

"Don't rightly know yet," Clint said, writing his name. "I guess that will depend on what kind of town you've got here."

"This is a fine town, sir, a fine town," the man said. "Of that I can assure you."

Clint put down the quill pen, accepted his key, and said, "I guess I'll have to make up my own mind about that, won't I?"

"Certainly, sir, certainly," the clerk said. "Have a

pleasant day"—he paused to turn the book over and read Clint's name—"Mr. Adams."

"Thanks."

"Adams?" the clerk said again, as Clint went up the stairs.

Clint didn't turn back. He went to the second floor, found his room, and entered. It was neat and clean. He tried the mattress, found it pleasing. He walked to the window and looked out over the main street. From this vantage point even the hard-packed dirt street looked clean. Maybe Virgil Earp, his father, and his younger brother had found themselves a nice, quiet place to settle down.

He left the room to go back downstairs and take Eclipse to the livery stable. As he crossed the lobby, the clerk was less enthusiastic than he had been earlier. In fact, he seemed to shrink back from Clint.

He found the livery where towns customarily put it, at one end of town. The liveryman was properly impressed with Eclipse and promised to see to his every need.

"Don't normally get animals that look like this," the man said. "I'm gonna move some of the stock around and give him the best stall."

"Suits me," Clint said.

"Speakin' of best stalls, where are you stayin'?"

"Hotel Colton," Clint said. "First one I came to."

"Also the best," the man said. "I ain't never heard nobody complain about the beds there."

"You know the town well?" Clint asked.

"I been here since before they decided to change everything," the man said. Clint thought the man could be anywhere between fifty and seventy. "Now we ain't a town no more, we're a city."

"And you don't like that?"

"I liked things the way they used to be," the man said. "I ain't a big fan of progress, mister."

"Can you tell me where I can find Virgil Earp?"

"Virgil Earp? Whataya want with him?"

"I understand he's set up shop as a private detective hereabouts."

"And you need a detective?"

"Maybe."

"Well . . . Mr. Earp lives over on West H Street. I think it's 529—no, 528 West H Street."

"And does he have an office?"

"Sure," the man said, "got one on Main Street, second floor, right over the hardware store."

"I must've missed it," Clint said. He grabbed his rifle and saddlebags and let the man lead Eclipse deeper into the stable.

"You want me to pay you now?" Clint called after the man.

"You can settle up with me when you decide to leave," the man called back. "Don't figure you'll walk off and leave this animal behind."

"Not bloody likely," Clint muttered, as he walked away.

TWO

Clint carried his gear back to his hotel room. He noticed as he went through the lobby that the clerk was not at his post. Either that or he was crouched down, hiding behind the desk. He didn't particularly care, so he didn't bother looking.

He left his saddlebags and rifle in his room and went in search of Virgil Earp's office. Along the way he came to a saloon, so he decided to get a cold beer first.

The saloon had none of the new smell some of the other buildings in Colton had. It smelled as if it had been around a long time.

There were only a few men inside, seated at tables and one standing at the bar with the bartender.

"What'll ya have, mister?" the bartender asked.

"Beer."

"Comin' up."

"Yer lucky ya found yer way in here," the man at the bar said.

"Why's that?"

"Only a few places in this city have a license to serve liquor."

"A license?"

The bartender brought the beer.

"Somebody's idea of improvements," he said. "No whorehouses, very few saloons."

Clint drank down some of the beer.

"Who'd come up with a stupid idea like that?"

"Politicians," the bartender said.

"Naw," the other man said, "politicians' wives. Dried up old biddies who don't want their men to have any fun, any pleasures."

"You got one of those of your own?" Clint asked.

"I did," the man said. "I left 'er."

"Best move you ever made, Lee," the bartender said.

"Don't I know it."

"You?" the bartender asked Clint.

"Never took the plunge."

"Smart man," the barman said. "What brings you to town?"

Clint decided not to mention Virgil's name until he found out the standing of the Earps in town. That family had a penchant for making enemies.

"Thanks for the beer," Clint said.

"Just one's enough?" the bartender asked.

"For now," Clint said. "It cuts the dust. I'll be back later."

"Remember," the man behind the bar said, "only a few places hereabouts can serve liquor, and we're one of them."

"And you're close to my hotel," Clint said. "I'll remember."

Clint left.

* * *

He walked to West H Street, then started looking for 528. He couldn't see the numbers, so he cut over to Main Street and started looking for a hardware store. When he found one he stopped and looked. Out in front were rakes, pickaxes, all kinds of tools for sale. The second floor had a big plate glass window that said "VIRGIL EARP, PRIVATE DETECTIVE."

"This must be the place," he said to himself.

"Lookin' for Virgil?" a man asked, from the doorway.

"That's right."

"Stairs are around the side." He was a big man, wearing a white apron over a bulging stomach. "You got some business with him, I hope?"

"You hope?"

"Only way he's gonna be able to pay his rent is to get some business."

"I see," Clint said. "Well, thanks for the directions."

"His brother's Wyatt Earp, ya know," the man called out, like it was a selling point.

Clint ignored him and kept going.

THREE

Virgil Earp was considering going over to his father, Nick's, saloon for a drink when the door to his office opened. Maybe this would be some business. Lord knows he needed some in order to pay his rent on the office. His wife, Allie, had been telling him to give the office up and work from home, but he'd been resisting the suggestion for weeks. It was only today he'd been thinking it might be a prudent idea.

He sat back in his chair, resting his aching shorter left arm on the armrest, and waited for his client to appear.

As Clint entered, he saw Virgil seated behind a pitted, wooden desk that appeared too small for him.

"Clint Adams?" Virgil said.

"Don't sound so disappointed," Clint said.

"Sorry," Virgil said, standing, "I thought it might be a payin' client."

"I think I met your landlord downstairs," Clint said. "He was hoping the same thing."

Virgil extended his right hand and Clint clasped it in

a handshake. Virgil was wearing a black suit that was frayed at the collar and cuffs. His left arm was noticeably shorter than the right.

"Have a seat," Virgil invited. He seated himself behind his small desk and patted it with his good hand. "Got this from the old schoolhouse. Looks a little small, I know, but . . ."

Clint looked around the office. It was also small, so the plate glass window looked even bigger. Other than two chairs and a desk there was a file cabinet, and no room for anything else.

"What brings you to Colton?" Virgil asked.

"I stopped to see Wyatt in San Diego," Clint said. "Wasn't heading anyplace special when I left there, so figured I'd drift up here."

"How's Wyatt doin'?"

"He's fine," Clint said. "Dealing some faro. He said one or two of you might be here."

"Three," Virgil said. "Little Brother James is running a boardinghouse, and Nick runs the Gem Saloon. He claims he serves the best Tom and Jerry in town."

"Tom and Jerry?"

"Yeah, it's, uh, eggs and sugar beaten together, then he adds brandy and puts the whole thing in some hot water."

"Yuck," Clint said. "Does he serve beer? I heard that the liquor licenses hereabouts are few."

"Oh yeah, he serves everything," Virgil said. "Wanna walk over?"

"Only if I can buy."

"Yer on," Virgil said, standing up quickly. His height also made the room seem smaller. "Let's go."

* * *

Virgil looked much more comfortable outside, as they walked to the Gem Saloon.

"So I guess business isn't booming," Clint said.

"Nope," Virgil said, "I ain't givin' Allan Pinkerton no nightmares, yet."

"Why didn't you just go and work for Allan if you wanted to be a private detective?"

"Couldn't do it," Virgil said. "Been workin' for myself for too long—that is, when I wasn't wearin' a badge."

"What about that?"

"Yeah," Virgil said, "there's some folks hereabout want me to be constable. I'm not sure I wanna wear a badge again."

"Yeah, I heard the same thing from Wyatt," Clint said.

"Tombstone is still too fresh in our minds, I guess," Virgil said. "I can still hear Morgan's voice, ya know?"

"I understand."

They walked past the little saloon Clint had already had a beer in.

"I had a beer in there," Clint said.

"Small place," Virgil said. "Not bad for just one beer. You'll like the Gem better."

"What's this about no whorehouses?"

"That's the way the prominent citizens of Colton want it," Virgil said. "I'll tell you what we do have, though. We got three newspapers, a telegraph, a Wells Fargo office, three hotels, two banks, churches and schools and cemeteries. And we got some telephones."

"What's the population?"

"About two thousand. Here's the Gem."

They crossed the street to a good-sized saloon with the word "GEM" above the door.

FOUR

The Gem Saloon was large, with many tables for both drinking and gambling.

"They've outlawed prostitution but not gambling?" Clint asked.

"I'm sure they're workin' on it," Virgil said. "Come on."

Virgil led the way to the bar, where a young man was tending.

"Hey, Mr. Earp," the man said.

"I told you, Billy," Virgil said, "it's just Virgil. Is my father around?"

"In the office, as usual, Mr. Ea—I mean, Virgil."

"Billy Kane, meet my friend, Clint Adams. Get us two beers, will ya?"

But the young man didn't seem to hear Virgil's order. He was staring at Clint.

"Adams?" he asked.

"Beer," Virgil said, lightly slapping the young man's cheek. "Pronto. And one for my father."

"Y-yessir."

Billy set three mugs of beer on the bar top nervously. Clint picked up two because, with his damaged arm, Virgil could only handle one.

Virgil tapped on the office door with his beer mug, and it was opened from the inside by Nick Earp.

"What the hell—" he said, then saw Clint. "Is that Adams?"

"It sure is," Virgil said, entering the office.

"And I've got something for you," Clint said, handing the older man a full mug.

With one hand each free they shook.

"Come on in and set down, boy," Nick said. "Whataya think of my operation?"

"Looks good," Clint said. "Always this dead this time of day?"

"Pretty much," Nick said, sitting behind his desk—a bigger and better desk than his son had in his office.

"I guess you're lucky you're one of the places with a license to sell liquor."

"Luck had nothin' to do with it," Nick said. "You gotta pay the right people."

"The respectable ladies of Colton think decisions are bein' made for the right reasons," Virgil said. "But it's the same old story. Money talks."

"So then, there have to be some whorehouses somewhere," Clint said.

"Oh, they're here," Nick said. "Are you interested in findin' one?"

"No," Clint said, "I'm just curious."

"You just passin' through, Adams?"

"Clint was in San Diego with Wyatt," Virgil said.

"How's the boy doin'?" Nick asked. "Still thinkin' about Tombstone?"

"Yep, still," Clint said. "Tombstone and Morgan. He's havin' a hard time dealin' with Morgan's death."

"Yeah, well, we all are," Nick said, "but ya gotta keep movin' forward."

"Oh, he will," Clint said. "It's just gonna take some time."

"Well, if you're lookin' for booze, girls, or poker, you let me know," Nick said. "If I can't provide it, I know who can."

"I appreciate it, Nick."

"What about you, Virg?" Nick asked. "Any clients?"

"Not a one," Virgil said.

"Maybe you should think again about that constable job."

"Yeah," Virgil said, standing, "I'll give it some thought."

Clint stood, shook hands with Nick Earp, and walked out with Virgil. They went back to stand at the bar and finish their beers.

"Sounds like Nick wants you to take that job," Clint said.

"Yeah, and he's thinkin' about runnin' for justice of the peace."

"He's not happy with the Gem?"

"Yeah, he's real happy," Virgil said, "but Nick's always lookin' to get happier. You wanna go and see James?"

"Sure, why not?"

"Maybe he's got a room," Virgil said. "We can get you out of the hotel, save you some money."

"What's James doing running a boardinghouse?" Clint asked.

"He don't wanna wear a badge, neither," Virgil said.

"I tried to get him to come in with me, but he says bein' a detective is too close to bein' a lawman. And he don't wanna work with Nick. That would drive any of us crazy."

They finished their beers and set the empty mugs down on the bar.

"Come on," Virgil said. "James's house is at the end of K Street."

FIVE

When they reached the end of K Street, Clint saw that James Earp's boardinghouse was the biggest house on a residential block. He hoped he would not be insulting the Earps if he turned down a room, but he preferred to be closer to where the action and activity were.

They mounted the front steps and Virgil stopped to knock. The woman who answered the door was in her thirties, and Clint didn't know where to look first, her beautiful, full-lipped face, her long luxurious black hair, or her obviously lavish body.

"Hello, Kate," Virgil said.

"Hi, Virgil. What brings you here? Allie kick you out and you need a room?"

She had a deep voice that reached all the way down deep inside Clint, who felt he was lost in three different ways now.

"I'm lookin' for James, Kate," Virgil said. "A friend of ours came into town today."

"Well, I think your brother is in the back, in his office," she said. She looked past Virgil at Clint, gave him a frank appraisal. "Is this your friend?"

"It is. Kate Violet, meet Clint Adams."

"The Gunsmith?" she asked. "That Clint Adams?"

"That's the only one I know," Virgil said.

She reached past Virgil to shake hands with Clint. She had a firm grip.

"It's a pleasure to meet you, sir," she said. "I knew when I started working for the Earps that I might end up meeting some famous friends of theirs."

"Really? How many have you met?"

"Actually, you're my first. Please, gentlemen, do come in."

Virgil and Clint entered and Kate led them through a comfortably furnished sitting room to the office in back of the house.

"Just down the hall," she said. "I'll leave you gents to it."

Both men watched her walk away.

"She's a little old for your brother," Clint said.

"Nothin' goin' on there," Virgil assured him. "Bessie would cut it off. But I gotta warn you. A lot of men have tried."

"I don't have much choice," Clint said. "That's quite a woman."

"Come on," Virgil said. "Maybe little brother can give you a hint."

They walked down the hall and entered the office. James Earp smiled broadly and stood up, sticking out his hand.

"I heard you were in town."

"How'd you hear that?" Clint asked.

James pointed to his wall, and Clint saw the telephone there.

"Nick's got one, too, only you can't see it in his office."

Clint thought this was the first time his presence had ever been announced by telephone.

Virgil once again explained that Clint was passing through after having spent some time with Wyatt in San Diego.

"This ain't exactly on the way," James said.

"It would be a little bit of a detour if I was actually going someplace, but I'm not."

"How long you gonna be here for? You'll have to come to supper."

"A couple of days, I guess."

"I'll tell Bessie to plan a big meal. Virg, you and Allie will come, too."

"What are you up to here?" Virgil asked.

"Paperwork," James said. "Worst part of runnin' a business."

"You sound like Nick," Virgil said.

"I'm better at it than Nick is," James said, "but not by much."

"How's business?" Clint asked.

"We're about half-full. You want a room? On the house?"

"I guess that depends."

"On what?"

"Clint saw Kate."

"Oh boy," James said.

"Does she clean rooms?" Clint asked.

"Not hardly," James said. "Kate's my partner."

"Bessie let you be partners with a woman who looks like that?"

"Kate and Bessie were friends first," James said. "We became partners later."

"Well, I don't think your partner's going to like you giving out free rooms, so I think I'll stay at the hotel."

"Closer to the action, huh? What there is of it. Colton's not exactly wide open."

"So I've heard."

"We'll let you get back to your paperwork, little brother," Virgil said.

"Have Allie talk to Bessie about supper," James said. "Probably tomorrow night."

"Sounds good," Clint said. "See you then."

Virgil slapped his brother on the back and then led the way back up the hall to the sitting room. Kate Violet was sitting there.

"James tell you I don't clean rooms?" she asked Clint.

"He told me," Clint said. "How'd you know?"

"It's what most people think," she said. "Don't feel bad about it."

"I do," he said. "I'd like to make it up to you."

"How?"

"James just invited me to supper tomorrow night," he said. "Virg and Allie will be there, which makes me the fifth person. Would you come with me and even it out?"

She stood up, smiled, and put out her hand.

"It was a pleasure to meet you, Mr. Adams."

He shook her hand. She turned and started to walk away.

"Is that a yes?" Clint asked.

She turned, smiled, and said, "I'll see you there."

SIX

Clint walked Virgil back to his office, and as they passed the hardware store the owner came running out.

"You have a client," he told Virgil.

"What?"

"A client, somebody who wants to hire you."

"Where?"

"I let them into your office."

"You did what?"

"I didn't want them to get away!" the man said, obviously thinking about his rent.

"So whoever it is, they're alone in my office?" Virgil said.

"Why? You got valuable stuff in there?" the owner asked.

Virgil shut his mouth, because the man had a point. What were they going to do, steal his desk?

"Okay, Mr. Daley, thanks," Virgil said.

"Maybe I'll get my two months' back rent sometime soon?" the man asked.

Virgil waved.

"I'll leave you to your business," Clint said.

"You got somethin' else to do?" Virgil asked.

"Well, no—"

"Come on up and hear what they have to say," Virgil said. "I'll introduce you as one of my operatives."

"Okay," Clint said, realizing that allowing Virgil to do that would impress the client. It wasn't too much to ask of him.

They went up the stairs and Virgil opened the door. A young woman leaped to her feet and turned to face them nervously.

"Are you . . . the detective?" she asked, looking at them both.

"I am Virgil Earp," Virgil said. "This is one of my operatives."

"How do you do," she said. "My name is Sally Quest. I would like you to find my sister."

"Have a seat, Miss Quest," Virgil invited. He walked around behind his desk and sat down. Clint stood off to one side, just behind the girl, so that she couldn't see him without craning her neck.

"Tell me about your sister," Virgil said.

"W-we live—lived in Nevada, in a mining camp, but she got tired of it and came to Northern California. I stayed behind, but after Pa died I decided to come and look for her."

"What's your sister's name?"

"Well, her name is Maybelle, but she told me she was gonna change it when she got to California."

"Change it to what?"

"She didn't tell me," Sally said. "She said she hadn't made up her mind yet."

"Did she write to you when she got to California?" Virgil asked.

"No," Sally said, "she said she would, but she never did. That's why I'm afraid somethin' has happened to her. If she was all right she would have written."

"How long ago did she come to California?"

"Oh, it's been . . . months," she said. "Almost a year, in fact."

"Excuse me," Clint said, "but do you even know that she got to California?"

She turned in her chair to look at him, so she wouldn't have to crane her neck. He noticed she had a very pretty, fresh face. He guessed her to be about twenty years old.

"Well, no, I don't. As I said, I never heard from her. You think somethin' happened to her before she even got here?"

"I was just asking a question, miss," Clint said. "We need as much information as we can get."

"I see." She turned back to Virgil. "Do you usually allow your operatives to interrupt?"

Clint smiled at Virgil behind the girl's back.

"When they ask good questions, yes," Virgil said. "It's possible my operative might end up workin' on this for me."

"Oh, my, no," she said. "You are the Virgil Earp who is related to Wyatt Earp, aren't you?"

"I am."

"Well, then, I want you to work on this personally," she said. "Money is no object. I'll pay whatever you want."

"Do you, uh, have money, Miss Quest?"

"Oh, my yes, lots," she said. "Between when May-belle left and Papa died the mine came in. Silver. Lots and lots of it."

"Lots?" Virgil asked.

"Oh, my yes," she said, again. "I have loads of money, Mr. Earp. In fact, I'm quite rich."

SEVEN

Virgil got a description of Sally's sister from her, wrote it down, and then they agreed on a fee.

"Will cash be all right?" she asked, opening the small purse she was carrying. It seemed that all that was in it was money. She pulled out a thick sheaf of bills and started counting them, laying them on the desk.

"Uh, that's enough," Virgil said, reaching out and pulling the bills to him. "I won't need more than that to get started."

"Really?"

"Yes," he said. "Put the rest away."

She did.

"You shouldn't be carrying that much cash around with you," Clint said.

"I don't believe in checks," she said, "or banks, for that matter, but Jason makes me use banks."

"Who is Jason?"

"Hmm? Oh, Jason Biggs, he's my lawyer . . . and he wants to marry me."

"Oh," Virgil said, "that's nice."

She wrinkled her nose.

"No, it's not. He's too old for me. He must be . . . thirty-five."

"Ancient," Virgil said, exchanging a look with Clint.

"I have taken a room at the Hotel Compton," she said, standing up. "I'll expect you to bring me any news."

"This could take a while, Miss Quest," Virgil said.

"I don't care," she told him. "As I told you, money is no object."

She turned, stopped when she saw Clint standing there, and said, "Nice to meet you, sir."

"And you, miss," Clint said.

She moved to the door with purposeful strides and left the office.

"That's quite a young girl," Clint said, taking her seat.

"Quite a young girl with lots of money," Virgil said, fingering the bills on his desk. "I think I'll go give my landlord at least one month of his back rent." He pushed his chair back.

"Why not both?" Clint asked.

"I don't wanna spoil him."

They went downstairs and gave the landlord his money, and then Virgil offered to buy Clint a steak.

"It's a little early for supper, isn't it?" Clint asked.

"Never too early for a good steak," Virgil said, "and I found a place that cooks 'em just right."

"Talked me into it," Clint said.

Virgil led Clint to a small café, where the middle-aged waiter greeted him by name, with a big smile.

"Meet my friend Clint, Jerry," Virgil said. "I told him

about your steaks, so we need two of 'em, and don't make me look bad."

"Don't worry, Mr. Earp," Jerry said.

As Jerry walked away, Virgil said, "Jerry's the waiter and the cook."

"How's his coffee?" Clint asked.

"Just tell him how you like it, and that's what you'll get. Oh, shit, you still drink that strong, black trail crap, right?"

"Strong as I can get it."

"We'll get two pots," Virgil said. "Jerry don't have a license to serve beer."

"You know," Clint said, as they waited for their food, "I was wondering something about your new client."

"Like how much money she really has?"

"No," Clint said, "like if her sister was heading for Northern California, why did she pick Colton to come and find a detective?"

EIGHT

Clint spent the evening in Nick Earp's Gem Saloon. While he was there, he discovered that the local law also drank there.

"Clint Adams," Nick said, at one point, "meet Dick Evans, sheriff of Colton."

"Adams," the lawman said, not offering his hand. "I heard you was passin' through."

Sheriff Evans, who looked to be sixty if he was a day, stared at Clint owlishly, as though he needed spectacles. In fact, Clint noticed a pair sticking up from the man's shirt pocket, but he didn't make a move to put them on.

"Not looking for any trouble, Sheriff," Clint assured him.

"Wouldn't be my problem anyway," the sheriff said. "I pretty much been replaced by a police department. The days of the sheriff are numbered. Mark my words on that. Gonna push us out soon."

"That's progress, Dick," Nick said.

Dick and Nick, Clint thought. The two men looked like they were friends.

"Well, there's one good thing about bein' pushed out," Sheriff Evans said.

"What's that?" Clint asked.

"Don't matter a damn now if I drink on duty. Nick, a whiskey. Adams?"

"Just a beer."

Nick signaled to the bartender, who reacted immediately.

"Whiskey for the sheriff, Billy boy, and a beer for Mr. Adams."

"Comin' up."

"See that boy there?" Evans said, indicating the young bartender.

"What about him?" Clint asked.

"Used ta be my deputy," Evans said, "but I got no need for a deputy now, so he's pushin' drinks."

"He's doin' more than that, Dick," Nick Earp said. "Give the boy credit, he wants to learn the business."

"Yeah, the saloon business," Evans said. "How long are you gonna be around once they stop you from serving liquor altogether?"

"That ain't gonna happen, Dick," Earp said.

"And that's wishful thinkin' on your part, Nick," Evans said, accepting his whiskey from Billy.

Suddenly, it was clear to Clint that the sheriff had started drinking long before he came into the Gem saloon.

"Sheriff," Nick said, "grab a table and relax."

"Don't mind if I do."

Evans staggered to a table and sat down heavily. Within seconds his head was down on the table and he was dozing.

"They let him keep his badge," Nick said, "but he ain't really been a sheriff for a long time."

"That's a shame," Clint said.

"It is," Nick said. "Believe me, Dick Evans was a good man at one time."

"Wait a minute," Clint said, "you don't mean Marshal Richard Evans?"

"Same man."

"My God," Clint said, "what happened to him?"

"Turned to the bottle when he realized nobody needed him anymore."

"But he was a federal U.S. marshal for years."

"New judge came in, they had words, and he was out," Nick said.

"What'd he say?"

"Actually, it was more what he did."

"What did he do?"

"Broke the judge's nose."

"I thought you said they had words?"

"That was Richard Evans's way of havin' words.

"So now he's Dick?"

"Figures he'll stay unknown that way."

"I figured out who he was."

"After a while," Nick pointed out. "Most folks ain't as sharp as you."

"So people don't know he's the famous Marshal Richard Evans?" Clint asked.

"No, and he wants to keep it that way."

"Well, I won't tell anyone," Clint said.

"What went on with you and Virgil after you left here today?"

"Virgil got himself a client, young girl looking for her older sister."

"Young girl?"

Clint gave Nick the quick rundown on who Sally Quest was.

"Well, at least he can pay his rent for a while," Nick said. "I keep tellin' him to come in here with me, but him and James, they gotta be their own men."

"Seems to me any man would be proud to have sons like that."

"I'm proud of my boys, believe me," Nick said. "I'd just like ta make life a little easier for them, that's all."

"Well," Clint agreed, "what father wouldn't?"

You, he added to himself, just happen to have the wrong sons for that to happen.

NINE

Virgil Earp walked into the Gem Saloon, spotted Clint sitting at a table, and waved. He walked to the bar, got himself a beer and one for Clint, then joined him at his table.

"Sent some telegrams," he said as he sat, pushing the second beer over to Clint, who had just about finished with the one he had.

"About what?"

"Checkin' out my client, for one," he said. "Lookin' for her sister in the others."

"Where'd you send 'em?"

"Seems to me if a girl was gonna set up a life in Northern California she'd do it in one of two places."

"San Francisco or Sacramento."

"Right."

"And the other telegram?"

"Friend of mine in Nevada," he said. "He'll check out her claim about the mine."

"So all your detective work is done for the day?" Clint asked.

"Yeah," Virgil said, "and I'm tired." He rubbed his injured arm.

"That hurt?" Clint asked.

Virgil dropped his hand.

"Not too much," he said. "It just kinda . . . aches sometimes."

He picked up his beer and sipped.

"It's just a . . . constant reminder, you know?"

"Of Tombstone," Clint said, indicating he understood.

"Of Morg," Virgil said.

Clint picked up his mug and raised it.

"To Morg."

Virgil nodded.

"To Morg."

They both drank and put their mugs down.

"You know, I don't believe you," Virgil said.

"What?"

"You and Kate," Virgil said. "How did you get her to agree to come to supper with you?"

"I think she's going to feel pretty safe among friends, don't you?" Clint asked.

"Still . . . I was starting to think she just didn't like men."

"Oh, she likes men," Clint said. "I can tell that from looking at her. You can always tell things about a woman just by looking at her."

"I know," Virgil said, "I can usually tell I'm in trouble by the way my wife looks at me when I walk in the door."

"You and James, you have your own houses?"

"Yeah," Virgil said, "and Nick has a room upstairs at our place." He leaned forward, drank most of the beer, and then stood up.

"What?" Clint asked.

"Speakin' of wives, I got to go. Mine will have supper waitin'. You want to come along? I'm sure Allie won't—"

"No, no," Clint said, "tomorrow will be enough for her. You go and give her my best."

"I will," Virgil said. "Stop by my office tomorrow, after you have breakfast."

"Right."

"And don't expect little brother James in here tonight," Virgil said. "His wife is even stricter than mine."

"Okay," Clint said. "Makes me even more glad I'm not married."

Virgil pointed at him and said, "You just might change your mind tomorrow night."

"Good night, Clint."

"Night, Virg."

Once Virgil was gone, Clint thought about the Earp family. Strong people, all of them, and they'd had to be, given the kind of lives they had led. After Tombstone—no, *in* Tombstone *and* after—their strength had been tested even further. They had come out the other side, but not unscathed and certainly not unscarred.

He had much admiration for the Earp family, especially for his longtime friend Wyatt. He admired them even more for their exploits in Tombstone—and for the lives they were leading after.

Wyatt was the one he felt the most sorry for. Wyatt thought that Morgan's death and the crippling of Virgil, were his fault. No amount of talk from anyone could convince him otherwise.

Clint wondered if Virgil and James knew just how guilty Wyatt felt.

TEN

Clint stayed in the Gem Saloon for some time, thinking perhaps he'd find a poker game, but one never materialized. Finally, he bid Nick Earp good night and went back to his hotel. As he entered his room, he remembered Sally Quest saying she was also staying in the hotel. He wondered where in the building she was.

He had removed his boots and his shirt, and hung his gun belt on the bedpost when there was a knock at his door. He figured it was going to be Virgil Earp for some reason, but still he grabbed his gun and took it to the door with him.

When he opened it, he wasn't looking at Virgil Earp, but at Sally Quest.

"Miss Quest."

"May I come in, Mr. Adams?" she asked. "I'm quite dissatisfied."

"If you don't mind entering a man's room, then come in," Clint said.

She entered, turned, and looked at him, as he started to close the door.

"I would like you to keep the door open, please," she said.

"All right."

"And put on a shirt."

"You're very bossy for a young woman in a man's room," he said, slipping his shirt back on. Just to show he couldn't be pushed around, though, he left it unbuttoned.

"What is it that is making you so dissatisfied, Miss Quest?"

"I feel I was made a fool of this afternoon by you and Mr. Earp."

"Oh? How's that?"

"You misrepresented yourself."

"How did we do that?"

"He said you were an operative of his," she said. "Neither of you told me who you really are."

"Does that matter?"

"I believe so," she said. "If I had known you were the Gunsmith, I might have wanted to hire you and not him."

"I'm not for hire, Miss Quest," Clint said.

"And you are not an operative for Mr. Earp," she said.

"That's not strictly true," he said, not wanting Virgil Earp to be made out a liar.

"Then you do work for him?"

"I would work for him," Clint said, "if he asked me to."

She held her hands in front of her very primly. Her dress showed off a very slender body. She seemed much too frail to have come from a mining camp.

"I'm confused," she said. "You just told me you weren't for hire."

"Not as a detective, and not to the public," he said. "I am not a detective, but if Virgil Earp needed my help and asked me for it, I'd gladly give it."

"For pay?"

"No, Miss Quest," Clint said, "because the Earps are my friends."

"I still wish I had been told," she said.

"Well, I'm sorry," Clint said. "I was really just a bystander while you explained your concerns to Mr. Earp."

"Well, he is Wyatt Earp's brother, right?"

"Yes, he is."

"Well . . . I suppose it's all right, then," she said. "Do you know if he's found out anything yet?"

"I know he's started his investigation," Clint said, "but I doubt that he's had time to find out much. I do have a question for you, though."

"Oh? What's that?"

Clint thought she was quite haughty for such a young girl.

"I know you said your sister was coming to Northern California," he said, "but why did you choose Colton to start your search?"

"Mr. Earp was recommended to me," she said. "I was assured that his business was not limited to Colton."

"I see. And who recommended him?"

"I'm not at liberty to say," she replied. "Besides, you've just told me you don't work for him, so I don't think you're entitled to that information anyway."

"Miss Quest—"

"I think I've found out what I came here to find out," she said. "I'll be going now."

She acted like she was waiting for him to try and stop her.

"What are you waiting for?" he asked.

"Well . . . I was told of your reputation with women," she stammered.

"And?"

"I just thought . . ."

"Oh, I'm sorry,' he said. "Were you expecting me to . . . try something with you?"

"I . . . well . . . Don't you think I'm pretty?"

"Pretty enough, I guess."

She bristled.

"What does that mean?"

"It means you're very young," he said, "and much too skinny for me, Miss Quest."

He went to the door and held it for her.

"Have a good night, Miss Quest."

She glared at him, looked as if she had something to say, and then stormed out of the room. Apparently, Sally Quest had thought she was too pretty for a man with Clint's reputation to resist. And what would she have done if he had tried to romance her?

ELEVEN

Clint was reclining on the bed, once again without his shirt, when there was another knock on the door. Sally Quest had only left about twenty minutes before. Could she be coming back? Once again, he took his gun to the door with him. He knew that the first time he left it behind he'd take a bullet in the gut.

When he opened the door, he half expected to see Virgil this time, but once again it was a woman—Kate Violet. She was smiling.

"Hello, Kate."

"May I come in?" she asked.

"Sure."

He let her in, closed the door.

"I came by earlier, but your door was open and you had a girl in here."

"A girl—she wasn't a girl. I mean, she wasn't a woman, she was—she is a client of Virgil's."

"A client?"

"She's hired him to find her older sister."

"Why did she come to your room, then?"

"Well, I was there when she hired Virgil and he introduced me as an operative. Apparently, here at the hotel she discovered who I really was, and she felt we played her for a fool."

"And did you?"

"No, no, nothing like that," Clint said. "I was just a spectator. There was no reason to introduce me."

"Are you going to holster that?" she asked, looking at the gun in his hand.

"Oh, sorry."

He walked to the bedpost and slid the gun back into the holster.

"Do you always answer the door with a gun in your hand?"

"Yes," he said, "always."

"Must be a scary way to live."

"You almost get used to it," he said. "There are a lot of men who have to live this way."

"Like the Earps?"

"That's one good example."

"James doesn't."

"James hasn't been through what Wyatt and Virgil have," Clint pointed out.

"No, I suppose not."

She was standing in the center of the room, a shawl worn over a simple cotton dress. Even though her arms were folded across her chest, he could see that she had a body that was bursting with sexuality.

"So, what brings you here tonight, Kate?" he asked. "I thought I'd be seeing you tomorrow night."

"I know," she said, "you will, but I thought we'd get better acquainted tonight so that we wouldn't be so awkward around each other—and the Earps—tomorrow night."

"Better acquainted?" he asked. "What did you have in mind?"

"Well," she said, "this."

She dropped the shawl to the floor, and then very easily let her dress drop after it. She stood incredibly nude before him. She had creamy white skin, which made her black hair look even blacker. Full breasts and hips, she had a true woman's body, which Clint had come to prefer to all others as he got older. There was nothing like holding a full-bodied women in your arms.

And with that he stepped forward and took her into his arms. They kissed deeply, and then she began to undress him. He was pleased to see that his observations about her had been right. She was extremely sensual *and* sexual, which he considered unbeatable.

"I knew it," she said, pulling his pants down. "I knew it when I saw you, and you knew it, too."

Naked, they fell onto the bed together.

Blocks away, in the Earp home, Virgil told Allie about the supper the next night.

"Clint Adams and Kate Violet?" she asked. "How wonderful."

"Now, let's not start thinkin' about matchmakin', Allie."

"Why not?" she asked.

"Because you know how Adams is about women."

"Ah, but he's never met a woman like Kate," she said. "What man could resist her?"

"Well, James, for one."

"That's because James has his Bessie."

"Well, me, then."

She poked him in the ribs and said, "You have me, why would you need Kate? Sit down to supper."

He sat down and she puttered around the kitchen, still talking.

"I'll have to talk with Bessie tomorrow morning so we can plan the meal. Will your father be coming?"

"No," Virgil said, "he'll be at the Gem, like always."

"Good," she said, "then there won't be an uneven number of people. I hate that."

She brought two plates to the table and set them down, then sat opposite her husband.

"You said Clint and Kate met at James's house?"

"That's right."

"Tell me all about it," she said, "and don't leave anything out."

"Allie—"

"Was there any heat between them?"

Virgil sighed, shook his head, and started to eat.

TWELVE

Clint held Kate's large breasts in his hands and sucked her nipples avidly. She moaned and held his head in place. At one point she laughed and began to rub her breasts against his face. She was playful during sex. Clint preferred to be serious when he was in bed with a woman. Playtime was for later. It was hard to kiss a woman while laughing.

"Wait, wait . . ." she said, pushing him away.

"What?"

"The light," she said in a whisper. "Douse the light. I like the dark."

"I want to see you," he said.

She laughed.

"You've had a pretty good look up to now," she said. "I like it in the dark. I want to see you with my hands . . . and other parts."

"All right."

He got off the bed, walked to the gas lamp next to the door, and turned it down. The room was then illuminated only by moonlight.

He went back to the bed.

*   *   *

Three men rode into town just as the light went out in Clint's room. There was no connection. They were strangers, had never been in town before, did not know that Clint Adams was there.

The lead man was Link Holman. He had a reputation with a gun, was a throwback to the gunman of twenty years ago. He kept count of the men he had killed. He knew how many he had ambushed and how many he had killed in a fair fight, face-to-face. He was forty-eight, and considered that his legend was not yet fully formed.

The second man was Dave Holman, Link's brother. He was thirty-four, idolized his brother completely, and would do whatever he said without question. They were built alike, tall and rangy, but Link had filled out in the shoulders over the years.

The third man was Derek Morrell. He was, for want of a better word, Link Holman's protégé. He was thirty-four, like Dave Holman, but he was bigger, harder, with a scar across his cheek that he'd gotten from a knife at an early age. Unlike Dave, he did not idolize Link, but he did admire him, and he knew he could learn a lot from him.

One of the things he had already learned from him was how to travel at night without your horse breaking a leg.

"There's a hotel, Link," Dave said.

"Relax, Dave," Link said. "First the livery, then the hotel."

"Then somethin' to eat?" his brother asked.

"This late?" Link said. "Not likely. You should still have some beef jerky in your saddlebags."

"Um, I ate that a few miles back."

"Then you shouldn't be so hungry," Link said. "You should be able to wait for breakfast."

"Unless . . ."

"Unless what, Dave?"

Dave Holman had second thoughts about what he'd been about to say.

"Never mind."

Derek Morrell made sure Dave saw him take a piece of beef jerky from his saddlebag, took a big bite, and then put the rest back.

Dave Holman hated Derek Morrell. Moreover he hated him because he knew that Link had a grudging respect for him. Dave Holman had been trying to earn his brother's respect for years.

Clint found that Kate had been telling the truth. She used every part of her body to explore him. Her fingers, her mouth, the tips of her breasts, even her toes. She was all over him for what seemed like an hour, and it felt like a massage.

When she was scraping his chest with nipples that were like diamonds, he decided to take charge.

He grabbed her, flipped her onto her back, and began to explore her the way she'd explored him—almost. His massage was a little more . . . invasive.

"Oh," she said, as he entered her with one finger. "Oh, my . . ."

She was very wet. He slid his index finger fully into her, then used his thumb to touch her clit at the same time. He circled it, used his thumb to spread her own wetness over her, up and down. If the light had been burning, he knew he'd have been able to see her pink glisten.

"Oh my God, Clint," she said, "what are you . . . Oh."
She caught her breath.

He kissed her belly, moved his tongue down through
her black pubic hair, inhaled her musk as she became
wetter and wetter, soaking the sheet beneath her.

THIRTEEN

Kate had a body a man could settle into, wrap around him, and enjoy, and Clint took total advantage of that.

Later, as they were lying together, their flesh sticky with sweat, she said, "My, how you do love women."

"You could tell?"

"Well," she said, "I was hoping it was me, but I think you're just a man who loves women. I've never had a man get so . . . involved!"

"That was you," he assured her, "all you. I do love women, but you're something . . . special."

"I don't care how many women you've said that to," she told him, "I like hearin' it. It's been a long time between men for me."

"Why is that?"

"Slim pickin's, mostly," she said, "but now that I've been with you, I'm afraid it's going to be even longer before the next one."

"I don't think I'm going anywhere for a while," he said, "so hopefully the next time will still be me."

"Well," she said, sliding her hand down between his legs, "speaking of next time . . ."

Dave Holman and Derek Morrell were waiting outside the livery when Link Holman came out.

"Now the hotel?" Dave asked.

"No," Link said. "I was talkin' to the liveryman and he tol' me about this boardin'house in town. We're gonna go there."

"A boardin'house? Why?" Dave asked. "A hotel's better'n a boardin'house. Can't take no whore to a boardin'house."

"Well, hereabouts ya can't take her to a hotel, either."

"Why not?" Dave complained.

"'Cause there ain't no whores in this town, that's why," Link said.

"What?" For Dave the situation was just getting worse and worse.

"What's so special about this boardin'house, Link?" Morrell asked.

"It's owned and run by James Earp."

"Earp?" Dave asked. "Ya meant . . . those Earps?"

"Yeah, Dave," Link said, "those Earps."

"Why can't Derek and me go and get a drink while you get us the rooms?" Dave asked.

"I don't want you walkin' around without me, gettin' inta trouble, Dave."

"I ain't gonna get into no trouble, Link," Dave said. "Derek can watch—"

"I ain't watchin' nothin'," Morrell said. "You're on yer own, Dave."

"This ain't a wide open town, Dave," Link said. "It's

tight, and I can't trust you. You're comin' with me. We can't afford no trouble."

"Why do you always think I'm gonna get in trouble?" Dave Holman demanded.

"You really want me to answer that question?"

"Yeah, I do."

"It's because you're too stupid not to get in trouble," Link told his brother. "You understand now, little brother?"

"I'll bet if Derek wanted to go for a drink you wouldn't stop him."

"Derek can look after himself," Link said. "You can't."

"Damn it, Link—"

"Shut up now, Dave," Link said. "The conversation is over."

That was what their pa used to say when he didn't want to talk about anything anymore. Dave hated it, and Link knew he did.

"Come on," Link said, "we gotta walk a ways to get to this boardin'house."

When James opened the door of the rooming house and saw the three men standing there holding their saddlebags and rifles, he thought of only one thing—finally, some business.

"Help you gents?"

"Yeah, we need rooms," the spokesman said.

"How many?"

"Two," the man said. He looked older than the other two.

"We have plenty of rooms," James said.

"That's okay," the older man said. "These two can share a room. They get along real good."

"Okay," James said. "Come on and we'll get you settled."

"Much obliged," the man said. "Sorry to bother you this late, but we just rode in."

"No bother," James assured them. "We're real happy to have you."

He didn't notice the three men exchange a glance as they followed him into the house.

FOURTEEN

". . . so Colton seemed like a pretty good place to settle," Kate said. "I met and became friends with Bessie, met James, and we ended up going into business together. Which reminds me . . . I have to get back."

She got out of bed quickly and parts of her jiggled nicely as she hurriedly got dressed.

"What's the rush?"

"I'm supposed to be in the house tonight so James can go home," she said. "Bessie'll kill him and me if he's too late."

"So we're still on for supper tomorrow night?" he asked.

"Oh yes," she said, looking in the mirror and smoothing her hair with her hands. She turned and faced him. "I think we've taken care of the awkwardness very nicely, don't you?"

He nodded.

"I think we handled it like proper adults."

She went to the bed to kiss him good night, danced away when he tried to grab her.

"Where's a good place for me to have breakfast in the morning?" he asked.

"We serve breakfast at eight," she said. "You could come there."

"I think James would wonder how I got invited. Why don't we leave that for another day?"

"Okay," she said. "There's a small restaurant about three blocks south of here, on this side of the street. They serve a great steak-and-eggs, and you look like a steak-and-eggs man to me."

"You've got me pegged right."

She stopped at the door, turned, and said, "That's what I thought the moment I saw you. Good night."

She was gone before he could return the "Good night."

In the morning he went looking for that restaurant and found Kate to be absolutely right. The steak-and-eggs was excellent as was the coffee. He also found Sally Quest there before him.

"Please," she said, when he walked in, "won't you join me?"

"Well—"

"Let's don't let the awkwardness of last night keep us from being civil," she said.

"All right."

He sat with her and had breakfast. All she had was an egg and some coffee.

"Is that enough to keep you going?" he asked.

"All I eat is enough to keep me going," she said. "A girl has to watch her figure."

Clint didn't think she had much of a figure. She could have used a few good meals.

"How long have you known Mr. Earp?"

"I've known his brother Wyatt a long time," Clint said. "Along the way I've come to know the whole family."

"How many are here in Colton?"

"Virgil's brother James and father Nick are here. Also, Virgil and James's wives."

"It would be interesting to meet them."

"Why?" Clint asked.

"What else is there to do here, while I wait?" she asked.

"You hired Virgil to find your sister," Clint said. "Why don't you go back home?"

"Back to Nevada?" she said, shaking her head. "Oh, no, I couldn't do that."

"Why not?"

She stood up. She was finished eating, while he still had half his meal left.

"Let me pay for your breakfast, Mr. Adams."

"That's not necessary, Miss Quest. I'll take care of mine and yours."

"You forget, Mr. Adams," she said. "I have a lot of money."

He sat back.

"You're right, Miss Quest, I did forget," he said. "All right, I accept your offer."

She put some money on the table.

"I hope you find a way to pass the time while you're here, Miss Quest."

"Oh, I will, Mr. Adams," she said. "I will."

She walked out with her chin held high. There was something about Sally Quest that bothered him. More than that, something about her he didn't like. But he couldn't put his finger on it.

He turned his attention back to his steak-and-eggs and asked the waiter to bring another pot of coffee.

FIFTEEN

When Kate had arrived late the night before, James told her about the three guests.

"Then we have to get Regina to make breakfast in the morning," she said.

"I'll stop and tell her on the way home," James said.

"It's kind of short notice," Kate said. "If she can't do something with her kids, then Bessie will have to come in and cook."

"Damn it, Kate, when are you gonna learn to cook?" James asked.

"Never," she said. "And even if I did learn, I wouldn't cook for the guests. I'm a partner, not a cook. I told you, I don't cook, I don't make beds—"

"Okay, okay," James said, "I heard it before. I gotta get home. I'll see you in the mornin'."

"Hey, hey," she said, "tell me about the new guests."

"Oh, yeah," James said. "They look like three hard cases—well, two. One's older, seems to be the leader. His name's Holman."

"That's it?"

"Well, they got in late, were tired, and by the way, so am I. I'll see you in the mornin', Kate. And don't forget about supper tomorrow night."

The next morning Regina showed up to cook, and Kate heaved a sigh of relief. She was a pretty black girl with four children who had many jobs around town. She was also a wonderful cook.

"Mornin', Regina," Kate said when the girl walked in. "I'm so glad to see you."

"Miss Kate," Regina said. "How many guests do we got?"

"Three?"

"Big mens?"

"I don't know, Regina," Kate said. "James checked them in."

"Is Mr. James here?"

"Not yet."

"I'll just cook up a mess of food, then."

"That sounds like a good idea."

Link Holman smelled breakfast and reacted the way a hungry man off the trail would react. He came downstairs and saw that the dining room table was set for breakfast. When he didn't see anyone else around, he went into the kitchen.

"Hey, Link. This is Regina. She's some kinda cook," Dave Holman said. "Look at this bacon."

Link looked at the pretty black girl standing at the stove.

"Is my brother botherin' ya?"

"No suh, he ain't. He's tellin' me how much food ta cook for you and him and yer friend."

"Is that a fact?" Link asked.

"Yes, suh," she said. "He's bein' mighty helpful. Would you like a cup of coffee until breakfas' is ready?"

"Sure," Link said. "That'd be swell."

She poured him a cup and handed it to him.

"Thank you . . . Regina?"

"Yes, suh."

"I'll wait in the dining room for our friend to come down. Otherwise, your kitchen will get pretty crowded."

"Yes, suh."

"So like I was tellin' ya," Dave said, "my mother used to put molasses . . ."

Link left the kitchen.

As promised, Clint went to Virgil Earp's office after he finished his breakfast.

"Hey, good mornin'. We're all set for supper tonight. Allie's excited. She and Bessie are plannin' a feast."

"That sounds good."

"I gotta warn you about somethin', though," Virgil said.

"What's that?"

"Allie's talkin' about you and Kate, ya know? Like a matchmaker?"

"Oh."

"So you better watch yerself," Virgil said. "She and Bessie will probably work on the two of you together."

"I'll keep it in mind. Had breakfast with your client this morning—and she paid."

"And why not? She has a lot of money, remember?" Virgil said.

"Yes, she reminded me," Clint said, taking a seat. "There's something wrong with that girl."

"Like what?"

"Well, she eats like a bird," Clint said, "but it's more than that. I just can't put my finger on it."

"She carries a lot of cash."

"Yeah, if she had given you a bank draft, I'd say let's check her out."

"But she didn't."

"You hear from the telegram you sent to Nevada?" Clint asked.

"I was gonna take a walk to the telegraph office in a little while to check on answers."

"I'll come with you."

They left Virgil's office and started walking to the telegraph office.

"So you got a bad feelin' about a girl because she carries a lot of cash?" Virgil asked.

"It's not the cash," Clint said. "I asked her why she didn't just go back home now that she had hired you."

"And?"

"She said she couldn't," Clint said. "And then she got nervous, got up and left the restaurant."

"Couldn't pin her down, huh? What do you think is goin' on?"

"That's my point," Clint said. "I don't know, but it's something."

"I tell you what," Virgil said. "As long as she's got as much money as she says she has, I don't really care."

When they reached the telegraph office, Clint waited outside while Virgil went in to check on his replies.

SIXTEEN

Derek Morrell had come down and joined Link Holman at the table by the time Kate came in.

"Good morning, gentlemen," she said. "Regina will be right out with breakfast."

"Thanks," Link said.

"Aren't there three of you?"

"My brother is in the kitchen with your girl," Link said. "I hope you don't mind."

"Um, what's he doing in there?"

"Just talkin'," Link said. "In fact, I think he's tellin' her how our ma used to make flapjacks."

"I see."

"He ain't doin' no harm," Link assured her.

"I'm sure he's not," she said. "We just don't usually allow guests in there. It kind of slows Regina down in her work, and we pay her by the hour."

"Gotcha," Link said. "Derek, why don't you get Dave out of the kitchen?"

"Yeah, sure."

"Thank you," Kate said, as the other man went into the kitchen.

As she started away, Link said, "Hey, what's your name?"

She stopped.

"Kate."

"You work here?"

"I own the place."

"Really?" Link sat back. "I thought I heard it was owned by one of the Earps."

"James," she said, nodding. "He's my partner."

"Ah," Link said. "Partner."

"No," she said, "not like that. He's got a wife. She's my friend, and he's my business partner."

"I see."

"I've got to get to work," she said. The man gave her the willies. He had a weird look in his eyes. "Paperwork," she added.

"Maybe I'll see you later," he said.

"Sure."

"Hey," he called, as she again started to walk away. "If I don't like breakfast, who do I complain to?"

"Yell at the cook," she said, over her shoulder.

"No word," Virgil said when he came out.

"From where?"

"San Francisco," Virgil said.

"What about Nevada?"

"Yes," Virgil said. "Miss Quest is telling the truth. She is the owner of the Quest Mine near Ouray, Nevada. She inherited it from her father when he died."

"And no reply from Sacramento?"

"No, not yet."

"How far are we from Sacramento?"

"It's a couple of days' ride north of here."

"Where is your San Francisco contact checking?"

"The usual places," Virgil said. "Whorehouses, saloons, gambling halls—"

"What about restaurants? Dress shops? We didn't ask Sally what kind of job her sister would look for."

Virgil looked out at the street, then at Clint.

"I guess I should've asked her that."

"Not too late."

"No, it's not. She's staying at your hotel, right?" Virgil asked.

"That's right."

"Listen," Virgil said, "the other way to go is you go to Sacramento and I go to San Francisco and look for her. Or the other way around."

"Whoa," Clint said, "I'm not one of your operatives, remember?"

"She has a lot of money," Virgil said. "I'd make it worth your while."

"You know, she stopped by my room last night and also told me she knew who I was."

"She recognized you?"

"No," Clint said, "somebody must have told her."

"Then she'd be real happy to pay for you to work on this."

"Maybe," Clint said, "but it's just a missing girl, Virgil."

"You told me you had nowhere to be," Virgil said, "and for all we know the girl could be in trouble."

They started walking toward the hotel.

"Let's talk to her again, see what else we can find out about her sister."

"Okay," Virgil said, "and you're havin' supper with us tonight. You can use the time to think over my offer."

"Okay," Clint said. "I'll think it over."

SEVENTEEN

Clint and Virgil entered the Hotel Colton and Virgil went to the desk.

"Hello, Mr. Earp," the nervous clerk said. "Can I help you?"

"I'm lookin' for one of your guests," Virgil said. "A young girl named Sally Quest."

"Ah, yes, Miss Quest. She's in our Presidential Suite."

"You have a Presidential Suite?" Clint asked.

"It's our finest and most expensive room," the clerk assured him.

"Is she in her Presidential Suite?"

"Uh, I don't know for sure, sir," the clerk said. Clint didn't know who was making the young man more nervous, him or Virgil Earp.

"Well, we're gonna go up and check."

"Of course, Mr. Earp," the clerk said. "Do you want to, uh, leave her a message?"

"I'll let you know when we come down."

"Yessir."

"Where is the Presidential Suite?" Virgil asked.

"Oh, uh, third floor, sir. Room 314."

"Much obliged."

Clint and Virgil walked up the two flights of steps and walked down the hall to room 314. There was no answer to their knock.

"Think she's in there, ignorin' us?" Virgil asked, pressing his ear to the door.

"Why would she?" Clint asked. "Suppose you had information for her about her sister?"

"You're right," Virgil said.

He knocked again. Still no answer.

"Okay, she ain't in there," Virgil said. "We'll have to talk to her later."

They went back downstairs to talk to the jumpy clerk again.

"Okay," Virgil said, as they reached the lobby. The clerk jumped, startled. "Just tell Miss Quest we were here lookin' for her and would like to talk to her."

"Yessir."

"Don't forget, son," Clint said. "Write it down."

"Yessir."

The clerk made a note. Clint and Virgil left the hotel.

They left the hotel, and Clint wondered what Sally Quest had found to occupy her time in Colton.

Sally looked around her and found the conditions in the restaurant deplorable. When the waitress asked her if she wanted something to eat, she suppressed a shudder and told her no thank you. But she did order coffee. When the woman brought it to her, she smiled, revealing gaps where teeth used to be.

She lifted the cup to her lips, smelled the liquor in it,

and put it down quickly. Now she knew why the wait-ress had been smiling.

When the man she was waiting for came in, she waved at him frantically, even though there were only two other people in the place.

"Miss Quest," he said, formally. His cruel mouth smiled, stretching the scar on his cheek.

"This is a horrible place to meet," she told him.

"From what I could tell," he said, sitting down, "it's a place nobody would see us. That's what you want, right? Nobody to see us together?"

"That's exactly what I want. I found him. I found Virgil Earp."

"So did I," he said, "so locating him ain't gonna be a problem."

"How about killin' him?" she asked.

"That's gonna be a little harder."

"Why?"

"Clint Adams is around."

"So?"

"Clint Adams is the Gunsmith."

"I know that," she said, "but you're a gunman. He shouldn't be a problem for you."

"The man is a legend," the gunman said. "He ain't gonna be so easy to take."

"What are you saying?" she asked.

"I'm gonna need more money," he said.

"What for?"

"For more men."

"I hired you," she said. "If you need more men you should hire them and pay them from your money."

The man laughed.

"That ain't the way it goes, missy," he said. "If you're

not gonna come up with some more money, then you can just take care of Earp yourse—"

"All right, all right," she said, "don't get so upset. How much more do you need?"

"Why don't we have a drink and talk about it?" he proposed.

"Here?" she asked.

"No," he said, "we could go someplace else."

"Where?"

He stood up and put his hand out to her. She slid her hand into his, and felt a slight thrill when she did.

"I have an idea," he said.

Sally Quest was a very skinny woman, but he liked his women skinny. Naked, her breasts were little more than bumps, but she had very large nipples, which fascinated him. In fact, they fascinated him so much that he spent a lot of time chewing on them. She moaned and writhed beneath him while his mouth worked on her and his hand delved down between her thighs. Her own hand was between them, stroking his raging erection. He was going to teach her some of the things she could do with that thing, but at the moment all he wanted to do was ram it into her and make her scream.

Sally felt the same things she had felt the first time she'd gone to bed with him in the town of Ouray, Nevada— revulsion and excitement. He was an ill-mannered, un-educated lout, but the moment she'd seen him she'd felt something down between her legs she'd never felt before.

Now, as he mounted her and pushed his huge cock into her, she gasped and wrapped her thin thighs around him. This had no effect on their business, she thought, none at all, but that was her last conscious thought as he started fucking her, taking her buttocks in his big hands and grunting as he took her. Her mind emptied and all she was aware of was the burning sensation inside of her . . .

EIGHTEEN

When Clint arrived at the home of James and Bessie Earp, he was the last to get there.

"Kate's in the kitchen with Bessie and Allie," Virgil told him, as he let him in.

"Where's James?"

"Still at the boardinghouse," Virgil said. "He's trying to get someone to stay there while he and Kate are here."

"Does he have guests?"

"Got three of them last night."

"Disreputable-looking men," Kate said, coming from the kitchen to the dining room, carrying a tray.

"Disreputable?"

"Well," Kate said, setting the tray down on the table, "they look like . . . well, outlaws."

"And you know what outlaws look like, do you?" Virgil asked.

"Maybe not as well as the Earps and Clint Adams do," she said, "but I do know when someone looks like an outlaw. Excuse me, I have to help in the kitchen."

"Do you want a drink?" Virgil asked.

"What have you got?"

"James has started drinking brandy," Virgil said. "I prefer whiskey or beer myself, but we'll have to take what we can get."

"Brandy will be fine."

Virgil was handing Clint a glass when the front door opened and James came walking in.

"Clint Adams," he said, approaching Clint with his hand out. "It's good to see you."

"James," Clint said, shaking the younger man's hand. "Quite a house you have here."

"A-frame, two stories," James said. "Solid as a rock."

"Unlike your boardinghouse."

"That drafty old thing?" James said, laughing. "It's very old."

"You want a drink, James?" Virgil asked.

"I sure do."

"What's this I hear about disreputable boarders?" Clint asked him.

"Three men, arrived last night," James said. "Looked like they were just off the trail."

He accepted a glass from his brother and watched Clint sip his.

"How do you like it?" he asked, anxiously. "I bring it in from back East."

"It's very good."

Virgil sipped his, made a face.

"Kate says the men look like outlaws," Virgil said. "Is that true?"

"They look like outlaws, or cowpokes, or drifters. All of that and more. But not bad enough for me to turn away some payin' customers."

"Good brandy, a fine house," Clint said. "Looks to me like you have plenty of money, James."

"Looks can be deceiving," James said. "I have to appear successful to become successful . . . Isn't that right, Virgil?"

"How would I know?" Virgil asked. "Look at my office."

"I told you to get yourself a decent place, big brother," James said. "Nobody's gonna want to hire a detective who has his office in a hole."

"I'm doin' okay," Virgil said. "Got a new client just yesterday."

"You did? What's the case?"

"A missing sister."

"Who's lookin'?" James asked. "The younger sister, or the older?"

"The younger."

"Does she have money?"

"Loads. She has a mine in Nevada. Silver."

"Big brother," James said, "this sounds promising."

"What sounds promising?" Bessie Earp asked, entering carrying some plates. Behind her came Allie and Kate.

"Virg has a client, a girl with money."

"Good for him."

"We were just sayin'—"

"You can finish your conversation over dinner," Bessie said. "First Clint has to say hello to me and to Allie. Come here, Clint."

Clint allowed himself to be hugged by both Earp women, and then bade a proper hello to Kate, who looked like the cat who swallowed the canary. Clint thought both Allie and Bessie were eyeing them suspiciously.

They continued to watch Clint and Kate during dinner. Clint managed to sit across the table from her, thinking he was safe, but he soon felt her foot—or what he thought was her foot—on his leg. She was playing a dangerous game with him.

And he didn't mind a bit.

NINETEEN

Link Holman, Dave Holman, and Derek Morrell were standing across the street from James Earp's house, watching it intently.

"This is more like it," Link said. "That boardinghouse is fallin' down, but this place is top-notch."

"The guy's got money," Dave said.

"Maybe," Morrell said.

"Whataya mean maybe?" Dave asked. "Look at that house."

"And like Link said, the boardinghouse is fallin' down," Morrell said. "If he had money, he'd be fixin' up his place of business, don't you think?"

"Maybe," Link said.

"So what do we do?" Dave asked.

"We still have to find out exactly how many Earps are in town," Link said. "So that's what we'll do."

"Ain't it a little late now to be askin' around?" Morrell said.

"It's not too late to go get a drink in a saloon," Link

said. "Supposed to be three or four with a license to serve. We'll split up and see what we can find out."

"What about whores?" Dave asked.

"If you want to question a whore—" Link started.

"I ain't wantin' ta talk to a whore," Dave said. "I wanna—"

"Ain't supposed to be a whore anywhere in Colton," Morrell said. "Besides, you wouldn't know what to do with one, kid."

"Now, wait a minute—"

"Dave," Link said, "I'm lettin' you go to a saloon alone to get information, and that's all. If you get yourself into trouble, I ain't gettin' you out. And if you get tossed into jail, I'll leave you there."

"Yeah, yeah, Link, okay," Dave said. "Okay, don't worry."

"Okay," Link said. "Let's go."

Link walked away, with his brother Dave and Derek Morrell bringing up the rear.

"You got any idea why we're really in Colton?" Dave asked Morrell.

"To tell you the truth, Dave, no, I don't. Link's playin' this on me pretty close to the vest."

Although Dave wanted to know what his brother was planning, he was secretly satisfied that Derek Morrell knew no more than he did.

Inside the house the six people had finished devouring a delicious dinner of roast beef, potatoes, vegetables, and biscuits. Allie and Bessie had cleared the table and had gone to get the dessert. They had insisted that Kate had done enough, that she was a guest and, therefore, did not need to assist them. For that reason Kate remained at the table with the men.

"James tells us you're right, Kate," Virgil said.

"About what?"

"The guests in the house. He said they could be outlaws, as you said."

"I told you."

"So, Kate, what do you think these outlaws are doin' in town?"

"You're the detective, Virgil," Kate said. "Why don't you find out?"

"Nobody's hired me to do it," he said. "You're the one who says they're outlaws. Give me your best guess."

"Well, maybe they're here to rob the bank," she said, "or the Wells Fargo station."

"Wells Fargo," James said, suddenly, "that reminds me, Virg. You know who's in town? Saw him earlier today on the street."

"Who?"

"Fred Dodge."

"I know Dodge," Clint said.

Fred Dodge was a Wells Fargo detective who was a friend to the Earps.

"Not unusual, since there's a Wells Fargo office here," Virgil said. "I'll have to stop in and say hello to him tomorrow."

"Mind if I tag along?" Clint asked. "I haven't seen Dodge in a while."

"Don't see why not."

Allie and Bessie appeared from the kitchen carrying plates of pie and a tray with coffeepot and mugs. Talk of

Fred Dodge and Wells Fargo was suspended in the face of coffee and peach pie.

"Peach?" James asked. "Why peach, Bessie? My favorite is apple."

"I know, James," Bessie said, with a smile, "but Clint is our guest, and his favorite is peach."

TWENTY

Clint drew looks from Bessie and Allie Earp when he offered to walk Kate home. Virgil and James Earp both seemed to be completely unaware that something might be going on.

Outside, walking back to town, Clint said, "You told them, didn't you?"

"What?"

"You told Allie and Bessie," he said. "They were throwing me looks all night. You told them while you were in the kitchen with them."

"Yes, all right," Kate said. "I told them." She shrugged. "Hey, women talk about men."

"And they don't think you're some kind of . . . loose woman?"

"They're my friends," she said. "They know how hard it is for a single woman to find a good man. And they don't judge me."

"Well, those are good friends to have."

"And you didn't tell Virgil? Or James?"

"I did not," he said. "I'm a gentleman, and a gentleman never tells."

She stared at him for a few moments, then said, "You know what? I believe you."

"You should," he said.

She grabbed his hand and pulled him along.

"Where are we going?" he asked. "Don't you live that way?"

"Yes," she said, "but your hotel is this way . . ."

Dave Holman turned the woman over, stared at her naked back and ass. He rubbed his rigid penis along the cleft between her ass cheeks. She was a thin girl, but she still managed to have big breasts and a nicely padded butt.

He lifted her onto her knees, poked his penis between her thighs.

"Whatchoo doin'?" Regina demanded.

"Ain't you never done it this way?" he asked. "From behind."

"You ain't puttin' nothin' in my behind," she told him, indignantly. "I ain't no whore."

"Not your behind," he said. "Look, just spread your thighs. I'll use my hand . . . see? Right there."

"Oh," she said, then "Oh! Dat's . . . nice."

"Now wait," he said. He slipped his penis between her smooth thighs, found her wet and waiting, and slid easily into her.

"See?" He moved in and out of her. "Ain't that nice?"

"Yeah, it sho is," she said. She lifted her butt higher, began to find his rhythm and back into him as he poked her.

They started out slowly, then he began to move faster

and faster. When Dave had met Regina in the kitchen, he knew he wasn't going to need to find a whore in Colton. This girl needed to be poked. He could see it in her hungry eyes. And he was right. He talked nice to her, complimented her, said how good her food was. When he helped her clean up in the kitchen he kept bumping her hip with his, noticed that she didn't pull away. Then, when they were drying dishes, he pulled her to him and kissed her. He liked the way she tasted and kissed her again. She responded, and soon their tongues were going at it.

"I ain't never been with a white man before," she'd told him.

"That's okay," he said. "I ain't never been with a black girl—but you taste so sweet, Regina."

She agreed to take him home with her that night, to a small two-room shack in a poor section of town, but warned him to keep quiet because of her five kids.

Now, as his breath began to quicken, she turned her head to look at him over her shoulder.

"Remember you gotta be quiet," she told him in an urgent whisper. "My kids is in the next room."

He gritted his teeth and said, "I remember."

But in the end it was her who made noise, crying out when he came inside of her, and from the other room a little girl's voice called out, "Momma, you havin' a bad dream?"

TWENTY-ONE

As Clint and Kate entered the hotel together, Clint saw Sally Quest starting up the steps.

"Miss Quest," he called.

She turned, eyes wide, and stared at him, then relaxed when she saw it was him.

"Mr. Adams," she said. "I just got the message you and Mr. Earp left me. Has there been any word?"

"No," he said, "but we did want to talk to you again."

"I'm really very tired right now," she said. "Can it wait?" She looked at Kate curiously.

"This is, ah, Kate Violet. She is a business partner of James Earp's."

"I see," Sally said, although she clearly didn't.

"Hello," Kate said.

"Can you come to Virgil's office tomorrow morning?" Clint asked Sally. "We can talk then."

"Yes, of course," she said. "I'll be there after breakfast."

"Good. Thank you."

"Good night," she said, looking at both of them.

"Good night," he said.

"Good night," Kate echoed.

Sally started up the stairs.

"That's Virgil's client?"

"Yes."

"The one with all the money?"

"Yes."

"She's very young to have so much money."

"Yes, she is."

"Shall we leave and come back?" she asked. "Or just follow her up?"

"Let's just give her a minute to get to her room," he said.

Clint turned and looked over at the front desk. The clerk was nowhere to be seen. As nervous as he was, Clint wondered if the man was hiding down behind the desk.

"Are you sure she has the money she says she has?" Kate wondered.

"She's got a lot of cash with her," he said, "and Virgil checked her out in Nevada. She inherited a silver mine from her father. She's got the money she says she has."

"So she's looking for her older sister?" she asked.

"Yes."

"Did Virgil check on that?" she asked.

"On what?"

"Well, you said she has the money she says she has," Kate said. "Does she have the sister she says she has?"

Clint stared at her.

"What?" she asked.

"You're a genius."

When Dave Holman got back to the boardinghouse, his brother, Link, was on the porch with Derek Morrell.

"Where've you been?" Link asked.

Dave grinned.

"You found a whore?"

"I found a gal."

"Who?" Link asked.

"That nigger gal who cooks," Dave said. "Regina."

"You been with a nigger?" Derek asked.

"Yep," Dave said, "and a sweet little thing she is, too."

Derek Morrell just shook his head. He'd never been with a black girl, and never intended to be. It just wasn't right.

"Did she happen to say anything while you were with her?" Link asked.

"I didn't give her much time to talk, if you know what I mean," Dave said, proudly.

Link and Derek stared at him.

"Say anythin' about what?"

"The house, about the Earps," Link said. "Anythin' that we could use."

"Use for what?" Dave asked. "Link, you still ain't told us what we're doin' here."

"I hate to agree with Dave," Morrell said, "but he's right."

"Don't worry about it," Link said. "You fellas will know what we're doin' in plenty of time. You gonna be seein' yer little nigger gal again, Dave?"

"If we're stayin' in town a few days, I hope so," Dave said.

"Well, if ya do," Link said, "see what you can find out about the Earps."

"Like what?"

"Just keep your damn ears open, boy," Link said. "Jesus, I don't wanna have to end up tellin' ya when to wipe your ass and when to wipe your nose."

"Okay, Link, okay," Dave said. "Take it easy. We just wanna know what's goin' on."

"When have you ever gone wrong listenin' to me?" Link asked them both.

"Never," Morrell said.

"Okay, then," Link said. "Just wait a while, that's all." Link turned and went inside.

"He was with a woman tonight," Morrell said.

"Him, too?" Dave asked. "Which one? The one who works here, with the big teats?"

"I don't know which one, but I can always tell," Morrell said.

"If he was with a woman it's gotta have somethin' to do with why we're here," Dave said. "He's my brother and I know that much."

"Well, he's right about one thing," Morrell said. "We've never gone wrong listenin' to him, so just do what he says and, sooner or later, we'll find out what the hell is goin' on."

"You don't have to tell me that, Derek," Dave snapped. "I know my brother."

"Yeah, okay," Morrell said. "I'm gonna take a walk and have a cigar. See you inside."

Dave watched Morrell step off the porch and walk toward town, lighting a cigar.

"Now what's goin' on with him?" he wondered aloud.

TWENTY-TWO

Clint wrapped Kate in his arms from behind and pressed up against her. Her body was still hot and moist.

"Are you staying tonight?" he asked.

"Do you want me to?"

"I'll buy you breakfast in the morning."

"Wow, that's an offer a girl can hardly refuse."

"Then you'll stay?"

"I don't know," she said. "I might need a little something extra to make up my mind."

Clint's penis was pressed against her ass and started climbing up her butt.

"Is that something extra enough?"

"I don't know," she said. "Oops, wait . . . wait . . . oh, it's getting there. Now it's big enough to be called a little something extra."

He turned her around roughly and kissed her, and now his cock was crawling up her belly. She reached between them and grabbed it.

"Oh yes," she said, "that's it!"

She mounted him, holding his hard penis so she

could impale herself on it. She started to buck on him, and put her hands up on her head so that her breasts jutted and bounced. She kept her hands there, closed her eyes, and just rode him. He watched her breasts with fascination, but eventually he couldn't wait anymore. He grabbed her hips and flipped her over so quickly that she yelled. He fell out of her as he did it, but quickly straddled her and slid his cock home again. She gasped as he drove in to the hilt, and then she started to laugh as he held her by the hips and plunged in and out of her . . .

"You don't laugh during sex," she said to him, later. "In fact, you don't even smile."

"Don't I?"

"You do before, and after, but not during," she said. "Why not?"

"Well, I find it hard to kiss while I'm laughing or smiling," he said, "and I love to kiss."

"Mmm, I can tell," she said. "Sometimes I think you like kissing better than breathing."

"Sorry," he said, "I love long, wet, slow, deep kisses."

"So do I," she said, "but you've got to warn a girl when you start one."

"What if when I start it I don't know how long or deep or slow or wet it's going to be?"

She pulled him down to her and said, "I guess I'll just have to hope I can figure it out before I suffocate."

They dressed and she begged off when Clint wanted to go to breakfast.

"I look terrible," she said, "and I'm all sticky. Need to go home, take a bath, get dressed, and go to work."

"I bet I can get you the day off," he said. "I know the boss."

"Ah, but you don't have the day off, remember?" she said. "You asked Miss Quest to go to Virgil's office this morning, and you have to be there, too, don't you?"

"I suppose," he said, grudgingly.

"So you go and have breakfast, and then go to your meeting," she said. "I'll see you later."

They didn't leave the room together.

"I have to try to hang on to my reputation somehow," she said.

He left, knowing she would sneak out later.

After breakfast Clint went to Virgil's office and found the detective sitting at his desk.

"Did you enjoy supper last night?" Virgil asked.

"Very much."

"Kate's a nice woman."

"Couldn't be nicer," Clint said.

"Allie and Bessie were hopin' you'd think that."

"You tell them I said it," Clint replied. "After I walked Kate home last night, I ran into your client."

"Where?"

"In the hotel," Clint said.

"Did you talk to her?"

"Briefly," Clint said. "She was tired, so I asked her to come here this morning."

"Well, she hasn't been here," Virgil said.

It was after nine.

"She said she'd be here after breakfast."

Virgil drummed his fingers on his desktop.

"How long you wanna wait until we go find her?" he asked.

Clint shrugged.

"Let's go now."

"You're on."

They left the office and walked back to Clint's hotel. They already knew she was in the Presidential Suite, so they went right up past the desk clerk.

When they reached her door, they knocked several times before Virgil tried the doorknob.

"It's not locked," he said.

"She's probably out," Clint said, "but since it's open, why don't we take a look inside?"

"What are we lookin' for?" Virgil asked.

"Don't know," Clint said. "Maybe we'll know it when we find it."

Virgil shrugged and pushed the door open.

"Smell that?" he asked.

"Yes," Clint said.

They both knew that smell only too well.

Blood.

"Damn," Virgil said.

"Better keep going," Clint said.

They walked through the parlor to the bedroom and found her on the bed. Her throat had been slashed, and she was very, very dead.

"Well," Clint said, "now you've got a real mystery to solve."

TWENTY-THREE

Virgil said he'd wait in the room while Clint went down to the clerk and sent him for the police.

"What about your friend, Sheriff Evans?" Clint asked.

"Might as well send for him, too," Virgil said. "Not that he'll have much to do once the police get here."

"Dead?" the clerk asked.

"Yes."

"Oh, my. Should I . . . go up?"

"Not unless you want to see a lot of blood," Clint said.

The clerk swallowed hard.

"Shall I fetch the owner?"

"Good idea," Clint said, "after the sheriff and the police. Now, get to it!"

"Yessir."

Clint went back upstairs, and found Virgil prowling the suite.

"Find anything?"

"No," Virgil said. "Thought there might be some sign of a man, but there's nothin'."

Clint stood in the middle of the parlor and looked around.

"Wanna have a look?" Virgil asked.

"Nope," Clint said. "I'll take your word for it."

"You know," Virgil said, "I'm not really a detective. I mean, I'm not trained or anythin'."

"That makes two of us," Clint said. "If you didn't find anything, I won't, either, so why don't we just wait for the police?"

"Fine."

"You got any idea who's going to show up?"

"No," Virgil said. "I haven't had my shingle out very long, so I haven't had anything to do with the police yet."

The first man on the scene was Sheriff Dick Evans. He came through the door, and stopped when he saw Virgil and Clint. Clint couldn't be sure if the man recognized him or not from the other night, when the sheriff was drunk.

"Virgil, what the hell," Evans said. "That pissant clerk said there's a dead girl up here?"

"The other room, Sheriff," Virgil said. "You better have a look for yourself."

Evans went into the bedroom, and came out looking pale.

"Damn, that's a young girl. Who was she?"

"Sally Quest, from Nevada," Virgil said. "She hired me to find her sister."

"And did you?"

"No," Virgil said, then added, "not yet."

"Send for the police?"

"Yeah."

Evans glanced around.

"I took a look around," Virgil said, "but help yourself."

"No point," Evans said. "When the police get here, I'll be done."

"Any idea who's going to show up from the police?" Clint asked.

Evans looked at him, frowned, then said, "They got a couple of detectives, but there's also a fella named Inspector James. He might show up when he hears it's murder. You fellas got any idea who did this?"

"Not a one," Virgil said.

"Adams?"

"No, sir."

"Shame," he said. "Young woman like that. Wonder what the reason was."

"She was carrying a lot of money in a little bag," Clint said.

"Is it still here?" Evans asked.

"Don't know," Virgil said. "I was lookin' for any sign of a man."

"Well, let's make ourselves useful and look for it," Evans said. "At least until the police get here."

They were still looking when two policemen in uniform arrived with their guns out.

"Hands up, gents!" one of them said.

"Don't be stupid," Evans said. "I'm the sheriff. These men found the body and sent for me and you."

"And you let them keep their guns?" the other man asked. "Sorry, Sheriff, but you'll have to leave, and they'll have to hand over their guns."

"I told you—"

"Look, old-timer," the first policeman said, "we got to do our jobs, so you just step out into the hall and wait for the inspector to get here."

Evans gave Clint and Virgil a look that said, "See what I have to put up with," and went out into the hall.

"Okay, gents," the first policeman said to Clint and Virgil, "let's have those guns."

TWENTY-FOUR

The sheriff turned out to be right. Inspector Raymond James arrived soon after the two policemen.

"Sheriff," he said, "what have we got?"

The inspector was in his forties, tall, wide-shouldered, with graying hair at his temples. He was more respectful than the two younger policemen had been.

"Murdered girl, Inspector," Sheriff Evans said. "Kinda gruesome."

"Who found her?"

"The two gents inside. Your men are holdin' them at gunpoint."

"Who are they?"

"Virgil Earp and Clint Adams. They're—"

"I know who they are," James said. "Mr. Earp is well known, and I know he has a private detective office. And Mr. Adams is also well known. Are they working together?"

"They're friends," Evans said. "Far as I know Adams is just passin' through."

"Okay," the inspector said. "Why are you out here?"

"Your men kicked me out."

The inspector shook his head.

"My apologies, sir."

"Like they said," Evans replied, "they're just doin' their jobs."

"Would you like to come back in with me?"

"Yes, thank you."

The two men entered the room, and found an odd tableau waiting for them, as if posed. The two policemen still had their guns out. Clint and Virgil were standing in the middle of the room.

"Officers," James said, "give these gentlemen back their guns, please."

"But, sir—"

"Do as I say," the inspector said, "and then go out into the hall and start knocking on doors, see if anyone heard anything."

"Yes, sir."

The two policemen gave Clint and Virgil back their guns and left.

"Gentlemen, my apologies," the inspector said. "The sheriff has told me who you are and, of course, I know you both my reputation."

He shook hands with both of them after they holstered their guns.

"Mind telling me about it?" he asked.

Virgil gave him the story of Sally Quest hiring him to find her older sister, carrying a lot of cash on her.

"And you checked on her story?"

"I checked on her story about owning a silver mine in Nevada," Virgil said. "That checked out."

"And does she, in fact, have a sister?"

"We're still checking on that," Clint said, to keep

Virgil from admitting that he hadn't asked that question, or thought of it.

"I see. And the money. Is it still here?"

"We don't see it," Virgil said, "or the small purse it was in."

"If she was carrying cash and paying for things in town with it, someone might have seen her, followed her back here, killed her, and stolen it. That sound right to you?"

"I saw her last night, in the lobby," Clint said. "She was alone, and was going up to her room."

The inspector turned and looked at the door.

"Doesn't look like it was forced."

"And it was unlocked when we got here," Virgil said.

"Then she let the killer in," James said.

"Looks like it," Virgil agreed.

"All right, gents," the inspector said. "You can go. Please come to police headquarters later this afternoon and I'll have someone take down a written statement from you both."

"All right, Inspector," Virgil said.

"Mr. Adams," James said as they started to leave.

"Yes, sir?"

"You said you were still checking on her story about a sister," James said.

"Yeah?"

"Does that mean that you're working with Mr. Earp in his capacity as a private detective?"

"Well, I guess it does," Clint said, "at least, on this one matter."

"Well," James said, "the matter seems to be over. She's my responsibility now. I hope you understand what I'm getting at?"

"We understand, Sheriff," Virgil assured him.

"Good," James said. "I respect both your reputations, and I hope we won't have any difficulties from here on out."

"I don't anticipate any, Inspector," Virgil said, then looked at Clint. "Do you?"

"Not a one," Clint said.

"Excellent news," James said. "I'll be seeing you both this afternoon, then?"

"Yes, sir," Virgil said.

"Sheriff," the inspector said, "why don't you walk them out?"

Clint thought the man had thought up the nicest way he could to dismiss the older lawman.

TWENTY-FIVE

Outside the hotel Virgil said to Clint, "How about we head over to the Gem? I could use a drink."

"So could I," the sheriff said, "but will they serve this early?"

"They will when your father owns the saloon," Virgil said.

"Let's go," Clint said.

They walked over to the Gem and knocked. The bartender, Billy, unlocked the door, saw Virgil, and let them all in. Nick Earp was sitting at a table eating breakfast. The other tables all had the chairs sitting upside down on them.

"Well, what bring you three here this early?" Nick asked.

"Murder," Virgil said. "Billy, whiskey."

"Me, too," the sheriff said.

"I'll take one," Clint said.

"Have a seat, gents," Nick said.

Virgil took three chairs down and set them upright on

the floor. They all sat with Nick while he finished his bacon and eggs.

"Who got murdered?" he asked.

"My client," Virgil said.

"Your only client?" Nick asked. "The one with all the money? Hope you got paid first."

"I did," Virgil said, "that's why I'm gonna find who killed her."

"The inspector wants you out of it," Sheriff Evans said.

"Yeah, I heard him," Virgil said.

Billy came over with three whiskeys, set them down, and then went about the room righting chairs.

"How did it happen?" Nick asked.

"Apparently," Virgil said, "she let somebody into her room and they cut her throat."

"Doesn't sound like she had very good judgment," Nick said.

"I don't know what this was about," Virgil said. "Did someone follow her from home and kill her, or was this random? Somebody in town who saw her with all that money in her bag."

"Why would she let them in her room?" Clint asked.

"Maybe it was somebody she made friends with since she got to town," Nick offered. "A man?"

"It didn't seem to me she was really looking for a man," Clint said.

"And she was a skinny little thing," Virgil said. "Not exactly the kind of woman who would attract attention on the street."

"Hey," Nick said, "men like all kinds of women."

"What about the sister?" the sheriff asked.

They all looked at him.

"Maybe the sister heard she was lookin' for her, sent somebody to take care of her."

Virgil looked at Clint.

"Thanks for bailing me out with the inspector," he said. "I never thought to check if there really was a sister."

"I didn't think of it, either," Clint said.

"I'd better send another telegram to Nevada and find out what family, if any, Sally Quest actually had."

He stood up, after downing his whiskey.

"And if she didn't have a sister?" Nick asked.

"Well, that'll give us another mystery," Virgil said. "What was she really after when she hired me to find a sister that doesn't even exist?"

TWENTY-SIX

Clint remained in the Gem to follow his whiskey with a beer. The sheriff decided to stay with him. Nick Earp didn't mind at all.

"But I got some paperwork to do in the office, so I'll leave you gents to it."

Billy brought them their drinks and went behind the bar to get it ready for business.

"Tell me about Inspector James," Clint said to Sheriff Evans.

"Ain't much to tell," Evans said. "Came from back East somewhere after they built the new police station."

"Who's in charge?"

"They got them a police chief," Evans said, "fella named Patrick—or Saint Patrick. I forget." He shrugged. "I ain't met him."

"Why not?"

Evans shrugged.

"I guess I ain't important enough for him ta meet," Evans said.

"The inspector seems to treat you with some respect," Clint said.

"Civil is what he is," Evans said, "which is more than I can say for most of them young lawmen—police officers is what they call 'em."

"So what are you going to do?" Clint asked.

"About what?"

"About this murder that took place in your town."

"Me? I ain't gonna do nothin'. I ain't a detective. Besides, that's all I gotta do is stick my nose in there and the inspector will stop bein' civil to me."

"You can just let it go?"

"Mister," Evans said, with another whiskey in his hand, "I been lettin' a lot go since that police department came to Colton."

"Yeah, but murder?"

Evans shrugged.

"That's Inspector James's business, not mine," he said, downing his drink. "I gotta go. Nice talkin' to ya."

Evans stood up and left the saloon. Billy left the door unlocked after the lawman had gone.

"I heard he used to be some kinda lawman," Billy said to Clint.

"Yeah, that's what I heard, too."

"Guess you've known some real fine lawmen in your time," the bartender said.

"I've known a few."

"Like Wyatt Earp?" Billy asked, sitting across from Clint with an eager look on his face.

"Look, Junior," Clint said, "if you're looking for me to tell you some war stories, forget it."

"I didn't mean noth—"

"I've got to go," Clint said, standing up.

Maybe Evans could sit on his hands while Sally Quest's killer walked free, but he couldn't.

Virgil sent his telegram, then stepped outside and stopped, looking up and down the street. There was a killer here among these people who were walking back and forth or riding by. Whatever Sally Quest was after, she was a young woman who didn't deserve to be killed that way. Nobody deserved it.

Virgil knew Clint felt the same way he did. They weren't about to leave this to Inspector James. They just had to figure out a way to find the killer without running afoul of the policeman.

TWENTY-SEVEN

Virgil and Clint met back at Virgil's office, where Virgil pulled a bottle of whiskey and two glasses from his bottom drawer.

"Someday I think all private detectives will keep this in their bottom drawer," Virgil said. "Especially if they have days like today."

He poured two whiskeys and pushed one to Clint's side of the desk.

"Okay," Virgil said, "I don't mind tellin' you I don't know which way to turn."

"Seems to me we have to retrace Sally Quest's steps, see who she met while she's been in town. Also find out from the desk clerk who, if anyone, visited her in the hotel."

"We know for a fact he's not always there," Virgil said. "Maybe the killer came in while he was off doin' whatever he does when he's not behind the desk."

"Got to ask him anyway," Clint said.

"So how do we retrace her steps?" Virgil asked.

"Leave the hotel, turn left or right," Clint said, "and start asking questions."

"Sounds like a lot of legwork," Virgil said, unhappily.

"That's what Talbot Roper has always told me detective work is," Clint said.

"Think we can get him to come here from Denver and solve this for us?"

"We don't need him, Virgil," Clint said. "You and me, we can do it."

"Glad to hear you sound so confident."

Virgil leaned over to refill Clint's glass, but Clint turned it upside down on the desk.

"No more for me."

"Okay."

He started to fill his own glass, but Clint said, "I don't think you should have any more, either."

Virgil looked at Clint, then sat back and stoppered the bottle.

"You're probably right." He stowed it back in the bottom drawer. "If we're gonna do some legwork, we might as well be steady on our legs."

"My thinking exactly."

"Then I guess there's no point sittin' around here mopin'," Virgil said. "Sally Quest may be dead, but she's still my client—at least until her money runs out."

Link Holman did not appreciate the fact that his brother Dave had gotten twice the amount of food on his plate at breakfast as he had.

Derek Morrell felt the same way, but he'd rather have gotten less than sleep with a nigger to get more.

After breakfast the three men went out on the front porch.

"You find out anythin' for us?" Link asked his brother.

"Nothin' much," Dave said. "Regina says that Kate and Mr. James—that's what she calls him—are both nice people to work for."

"Anythin' goin' on between them two?" Link asked.

"I asked her that," Dave said, seemingly proud that he had thought of it. "She says they're just partners, that Mr. James is a happily married man."

"And Kate?"

"Regina says she thinks Kate is keepin' company—that's what she called it—with Clint Adams."

"Well," Link said, "you finally came up with somethin' worth knowin'."

"I did?"

"Yeah."

"What are we gonna do with that?" Morrell asked.

"I don't know yet," Link said, "but I'll think of somethin'."

TWENTY-EIGHT

Clint and Virgil decided to split Pennsylvania Street between them. They started at the hotel. Clint went left, Virgil went right. They were going to ask people—shopkeepers, restaurant owners—if anyone had seen or met Sally Quest during the past few days.

Clint stopped into every store and restaurant he thought someone like Sally Quest would stop in—a dress shop, a hat store, a small café. He described Sally to the owners and employees, but nobody recognized her. However, one of the customers heard him talking and spoke up.

"I saw that girl," the man said.

Clint turned away from the café owner and looked at the customer who had spoken. He was a man in his early forties, cheaply dressed, having a small meal, probably what he could afford.

"Where did you see her?" Clint asked.

"Well . . . it was in a little restaurant over on Poplar Street."

"A saloon?"

"No, a café, I guess, but not the kind of place you think you'd see a lady," the man said.

"Why not?"

"It's not a very good section of town."

"When did you see her?"

"Last night."

"Can you tell me how to get to this place?"

"Sure, mister."

Clint listened to the man's directions, then turned to the waiter and said, "Give this man anything he wants to eat," and handed the waiter some money.

"Thanks, mister!"

As he left, he heard the man ordering a steak with all the trimmings.

Clint followed the man's directions and saw what he meant. As he got closer, the neighborhood changed drastically. Not the kind of area you'd expect to see a Sally Quest in. Run-down hotels, boarded up stores, and—despite what he'd been told about no bordellos—street prostitutes.

He came to the restaurant and entered. The first thing he noticed was an outline on the floor of where a bar used to stand. Obviously, this used to be a saloon, but they didn't get a license to serve liquor, so now they called themselves a restaurant.

"Somethin' ta eat, mister?" a waitress asked. She was young, but when she smiled she had two teeth missing, and the others were yellow.

"No, thanks," he said. "I'm not hungry."

He looked around. Apparently, no one else was hungry, either. Some of the tables were taken, the people sitting with what looked like coffee cups in front of them.

"Maybe you want . . . something else?" she asked.

He looked at her, but she wasn't being flirtatious. He looked around again. People were drinking their coffee with quiet relish.

"I'll take a table, and a . . . cup of coffee."

"This way."

She led him to a table, then disappeared into the kitchen—or what he assumed was the kitchen. When she returned she set a coffee cup in front of him.

He stared down at the cup, then sniffed it. He'd been right. They were serving whiskey without a license, using coffee cups.

"Anythin' else?" she asked.

"Yes," he said, "I'm looking for anyone who saw a girl in here last night, a blond girl, very young, very thin—"

"And snooty?"

"That's her."

"Yeah, she was here," the waitress said. "She acted like we all smelled and she was the queen of . . . I dunno, somethin'."

Yep, he thought, that was Sally Quest.

"Was she here alone?"

"Well, she got here alone," the waitress said, "took a table, ordered coffee—real coffee—and waited."

"And then?"

"A man came in and sat with her."

"Then what happened?"

"They talked awhile, and then they left together."

"Was she waiting for the man, or did he just sit down with her?"

"No, I got the impression she came here to wait for him."

"Can you describe him?"

She could, and she did.

TWENTY-NINE

Clint went back to the Hotel Colton and found the clerk behind the desk.

"I have a question for you," he said to the young man. "If you lie to me, I'll drag you over this desk. You understand?"

The man swallowed and said, "Yessir."

"The girl who was killed," Clint said. "Did she come here with a man last night?"

"No, sir."

"Are you sure?"

"Yessir."

Clint studied the young man, who seemed nervous and afraid. He didn't think the clerk was lying to him.

"Did a man ever come here looking for her? Or did a man ever visit her in her room?"

"No, sir."

"Are you sure?"

"I'm positive, sir."

"Are you the only clerk who works here?"

"No, sir."

"I've never seen another one."

"I work here m-most of the time."

"And the times you're not here, and the desk is empty? Like last night?"

"I, um, sometimes slip into the back for a, um, drink . . . sir."

"A long drink?"

"Well . . . sometimes I have too much and I, um, fall asleep."

"And your boss doesn't know?"

"No, sir," the man said. "You won't tell 'im, will you?"

"Not as long as you continue to tell me the truth."

"I will, sir. I swear."

"Has anyone from the police been here to talk to you yet?"

"I, uh, talked with the inspector this morning."

"And what did you tell him?"

The man hesitated, then said, "You won't kill me?"

"Not if you tell me the truth."

"Well, he asked me the same thing you did, about men comin' here to see Miss Quest."

"Yeah?"

"I-I told him the only men I saw was you and Mr. Earp."

The young man shrank back, as if he was expecting Clint to yank him over the desk.

"Okay," Clint said, "it's okay. Forget it."

The man relaxed. Clint turned and left without saying anything else to him. As he stepped outside, he saw Virgil walking toward the hotel.

"What'd you find out?" Virgil asked him.

Clint told him, then asked, "How about you?"

"Nothin' about anybody seein' her, but I stopped at the telegraph office."

"And?"

"My man in Nevada says Sally Quest was an only child," Virgil said. "No sister, no siblings, so nothin'."

"So what the hell was her game?" Clint said. "What was she after?"

"That description you got of the man she met?" Virgil asked. "That mean anything to you?"

"No, you?"

"No," Virgil said, "but I guess we're gonna have to find him."

THIRTY

Clint and Virgil were about to split up again when two uniformed policemen approached them. They were the same two who had come to Sally's room.

"Excuse us, gents," one of them said, "but the inspector would like you to come to the station and make your statements."

Clint looked at Virgil. "Oh, we forgot about those," he said.

"Damn," Virgil said. "Tell the inspector we'll be there presently."

"No," the other policeman said, "he sent us here to get you and bring you back."

Clint could see the man's words rankled Virgil, but he stepped between them.

"Okay, Officer," he said, putting his hand on Virgil's good arm, "lead the way. We'll come along."

The policemen eyed them both cautiously before turning their backs.

"We might as well get this done," Clint said to Virgil, "so we can get on with our business."

Virgil hesitated, then nodded. He and Clint followed the two policemen.

The police station was a brand-new, three-story brick building. The two policemen walked Clint and Virgil past the front desk and down a couple of hallways, until they reached Inspector James's office.

"Thank you for coming in, gentlemen," he said, rising from behind his desk.

"We're sorry you had to send for us, Inspector," Clint said. "We did intend to come in, but we got kind of . . . caught up."

"That's all right," James said. "I wonder if you'd make your statements separately, so I can talk to you each in turn out here."

"Sure," Clint said.

"I'll go first," Virgil said.

"Thank you," the inspector said, again. "Mr. Adams, would you have a seat?"

"Sure," Clint said. While Virgil left to give his statement, the inspector sat, and Clint sat opposite him.

"It seems to me you and Mr. Earp have been busy this morning and afternoon," the inspector said.

"Why would you say that?"

"Well, as you said, it slipped your mind to come in and make your statements," James said. "Has Mr. Earp taken another case so soon?"

"Not that I know of," Clint said, "but then he doesn't check in with me before he takes a case on."

"And you weren't together all day?"

"No," Clint said, "we each had our own business to take care of."

James frowned.

"I understood that you were just passing through Colton," he said.

"That's right."

"Then what business would you have had to take care of?"

"That was just a figure of speech, Inspector," Clint said. "All I meant was, we each had something of our own to do."

"I see."

"How has your investigation been going?"

"Slowly, I'm afraid," the inspector said.

"That's too bad."

"I'm afraid the young lady may have chosen to bring the wrong man to her room."

"So you believe her death was the result of a random meeting?"

"What do you think?"

"Me?" Clint asked. "Inspector, you made it very clear to Mr. Earp and me that you didn't want us thinking about this."

"And that was enough to dissuade you?"

"Well, I don't know about Virgil," Clint said, "but I try to be as law-abiding as I can."

"With your reputation, I'm sure that's wise," the inspector said. "Still, I can't help thinking you'd have some thoughts on the subject."

It occurred to Clint that the inspector might actually be asking for help.

"Well . . . I don't really believe she came all this way and was the victim of random violence," Clint said. "After all, we're in California, not the Wild West. You are more . . . sophisticated here, aren't you? Much more modern?"

"Supposedly," the inspector said, "but I'm not at all sure that everyone here got that message."

"I understand you're from back East, Inspector."

"I spent some time with both the Philadelphia Police Department and then the St. Louis police. I just sort of worked my way west."

"And how are you finding it here?"

"I believe it is a sort of combination of what's going on in the East and the West."

That was as good a description as any Clint had heard to describe California. After all, how much farther west could you get? And yet when people talked about the "West," they obviously were not talking about California.

"Well, I'm not a detective, Inspector, so I don't know what help I could be to you," Clint said. "My plan was to simply stay out of your way."

"I suppose that is a wise plan of action," the inspector said.

Behind him Clint heard Virgil enter the room.

"Ah, Mr. Earp. Finished already?"

"I didn't have much to say."

"So I guess it's my turn," Clint said, getting to his feet.

As he left the office, he heard the inspector say to Virgil, "Mr. Earp, will you have a seat?"

THIRTY-ONE

Clint finished making his statement, and instead of going back to the inspector's office, he chose to wait outside for Virgil.

When Virgil came out, they compared notes and found that the inspector had taken the same tack with both of them, and that they had each handled it in a similar manner.

"I told him my client was dead and that it was his job to find out who killed her, not mine," Virgil said.

"I pretty much said the same thing," Clint said.

"Where were we before we got hauled over here?" Virgil asked.

"The man Sally met at that restaurant I went to," Clint said. "We've got a description."

"But we don't know if he's from here or was just passin' through," Virgil pointed out.

"Let's check the livery stables in town," Clint said. "Maybe he killed her last night and left town this morning."

"Don't you think the police would've checked on that already?"

"You'd think so, wouldn't you?" Clint asked.

They spent the rest of the day finding any place a man could've left a horse and then checking on men who had left town that morning. They found three cases of men leaving town, but none matched the description Clint had been given by the gap-toothed waitress.

"So he's still in town," Virgil said. "Whether he's passin' through or he lives here, he's still here."

"So all we have to do is sniff him out from among the two thousand people who live here, plus visitors," Clint said.

"Well, hey," Virgil said, "luckily there's two of us."

"What about James?" Clint asked. "Maybe he'd like to help."

"And then there'd be three," Virgil said. "That oughtta get it done a lot sooner, right?"

"Virgil, if you don't want to—"

"Hey, hey," Virgil Earp said, "O.K. Corral, remember? At least nobody's tryin' to kill us."

THIRTY-TWO

Clint and Virgil walked to James's boardinghouse. Meanwhile, Link and Dave Holman, along with Derek Morrell, left the boardinghouse to walk over to Philadelphia Street and the business center of Colton. The two groups took different routes, and did not pass each other along the way.

"Why ain't we out lookin' for Virgil Earp?" Dave asked.

"Why would we do that?" Link asked.

"I figure that must be why we're here," his brother said. "To kill an Earp, and if it was James, we coulda done that as soon as we got here and he let us into his boardinghouse."

"Idiot," Link said. "When he let us in, we didn't know who he was."

"Okay, so we coulda dunnit when we found out who he was," Dave said. "My point is, we're here ta kill Virgil Earp."

"That wouldn't be very smart," Morrell said.

"Why not?" Dave asked.

"Look what happened in Tombstone, after his brother Morgan was killed and Virgil was crippled. He hunted them all down and killed them, even Ringo."

"Doc Holliday got Ringo," Dave said.

"That's what you say."

"Virgil Earp ain't got no Doc Holliday here in town," Dave said.

"You *are* an idiot," Link said.

"Why?"

"What would Virgil Earp need with a Doc Holliday?" Link asked. "He's got the Gunsmith."

"You wanna go up against the Gunsmith, Dave?" Morrell asked.

"That wouldn't be my job, Derek," Dave said. "It would be yours. Unless you're afraid of Clint Adams?"

"Link is right," Morrell said.

"About what?" Dave asked, frowning.

"You are an idiot."

"Oh yeah? How about—"

"Shut up," Link said, and then added, "idiot."

When Clint and Virgil arrived at the bardinghouse, they were admitted by Kate.

"All alone?" Clint asked, as Kate let them in.

"James is in the office, doing paperwork," she said. "Are you here to see him or me?"

"Him, I'm afraid," Virgil said.

She looked at Clint and asked, "Both of you?"

"Both of us," Clint said.

"Well, go ahead, then," she said. "I'm sure he'll welcome the distraction."

They headed back to the office. James was sitting behind his desk, poring over some papers.

"Hey, little brother," Virgil said. "Wanna play detective?"

James sat back, looked up at them, and rubbed his face over his face.

"What are you talkin' about?"

"We could use your help."

James looked at Clint. "He's makin' a detective out of you, too?"

Clint shrugged. "I've got nothing better to do right now."

James looked down at his paperwork, then at his brother.

"You know, neither do I," he said. "What's on your mind?"

THIRTY-THREE

They sat in the parlor and had coffee that Kate was nice enough to serve them.

"Four mugs?" James asked.

She sat down on the sofa next to Clint.

"I served the coffee, so I get to stay."

James looked at Virgil.

"It's okay with me," Virgil said.

"Fine," James said. "What do you want me to do?"

"We have a man's description," Virgil said. "He was seen with Sally Quest the afternoon she was killed. We need to find him."

"And how do we go about that?" James asked.

"Simple," Clint said. "We walk around town and ask people if they've seen him."

"That's simple?" James asked. "That could take forever. I think I'd rather go back and do my paperwork."

"Really?" Kate asked. "You hate paperwork."

"You're right," James said. "At least this way I'll be outside. Okay, so what do we do? Split the city up among the three of us?"

"Four of us," Kate said.

"No," Clint said.

"Why not?"

"Because you might be the one to find him," Clint said. "He's already killed one woman."

"What makes you think this man is the killer?" she asked. "Maybe the killer is a woman."

"This is the last person she was seen with," Clint said. "It's all we have to go on, and I don't want you finding him."

"If I find him, I won't approach him," she said. "I'm not that stupid. I'll just see where he goes and then tell you and Virgil."

"We can cover more ground with four of us, Clint," Virgil said.

"I can testify to the fact that she's not stupid," James said, then added, "at least, most of the time."

"James!" she said.

All three of them were watching Clint, as if the decision were just his.

"Okay, fine," he said. "But make sure you don't go anywhere near him."

"I promise." She crossed her heart.

"All right," James said. "What's this fella's description?"

"He's a big guy, rough-lookin'—" Virgil started.

"Oh, fine, that narrows it down," James said.

"Quiet, James," Kate said.

"In his mid-thirties," Virgil went on. "He was wearing worn trail clothes, a gun on his right hip—oh, and he had a scar on his left cheek."

"Hell," James said, "that could be Clint."

"Except for the mid-thirties part," Virgil pointed out.

"How big?" Kate asked.

"The scar?" Virgil replied.

"No, how big is the man?"

"She said he was big, with wide shoulders—oh, and she said he had a cruel mouth."

"Only a woman would say that" James said.

"Only a woman would see it," Kate said. "What else?"

"That's it," Clint said. "Now we hit the streets and see if we can find anybody who's seen him."

Kate stood up, seemed agitated.

"What is it?" Clint asked.

"I don't think we have to go out," she said.

"Why not?" Virgil asked.

"James," she said, "the three men staying here."

"What about them?"

"Have you taken a good look at them?"

"No," James admitted. "They came in late, I gave them their rooms . . . I don't think I've seen them since."

"Well, I have," she said, "and that description matches one of them."

Clint stood up.

"Are you sure?"

"Positive," she said. "Right down to the cruel mouth and the scar."

"Do we have names?" Virgil asked.

"I only know first names," she said, "and I don't know which is which, really. I just remember Link, Dave, and . . . Derek."

"Ring a bell?" Clint asked Virgil.

"No."

Clint looked at Kate.

"Are they in their rooms?"

"No," she said. "They left just a little while ago."

"All three?" Clint asked.

"Yes."

"All right," Clint said, "now you stay out of it, Kate. There's three of them, and we'll probably have to deal with all of them."

"So now we go out and look for them?" James asked.

"No," Clint said, "we'll just wait right here for them to come back."

"Shouldn't we send for the police?" Kate asked.

"No," Virgil said. "This is for us to do. James, get your gun and strap it on."

"So now I don't get to go out?" James complained.

"Kate," Clint said, "do you have someplace you can go for a while?"

"I can go home."

"I thought you lived here."

"No," she said, "sometimes I stay here, but I have a small place."

"Then go to it," Clint said.

"But . . . why not send for the police?"

"We don't know if these three men have done anything," Clint said. "We don't know that the man we're looking for did anything but have a cup of coffee with Sally Quest."

"Then let the police ask them."

"Kate," Virgil said, "the girl was my client—still is. This is for me to do."

"I don't understand that."

"You don't have to," Virgil told her. "You just have to go someplace and be safe."

"Virgil—"

"James," Clint said, "walk her out."

"Come on, Kate," James said. "You're not gonna win with these two."

"If you get killed, I won't have anything else to do with any of the three of you," she said, as James ushered her out.

When James returned, Clint said, "Show us their rooms, James. Let's see what we can find out."

THIRTY-FOUR

James took them up to the two rooms the three men were inhabiting. Saddlebags were all they found, and not much in them besides an extra shirt and, in one case, a knife and an extra gun.

"Nothin' to identify them," Virgil said. "Don't most men carry a letter or somethin' with their name on it?"

"Do you, when you're on the trail?" James asked.

"No," Virgil said.

"Neither do I," James said.

"Me, neither."

James walked over to stand by the window.

"James!" Virgil snapped. "Move away from the window!"

"You think somebody's gonna take a shot at me?" James asked.

"Maybe not," Virgil said, "but somebody might see you."

"Gotcha," James said, and moved away—but, of course, it was too late.

* * *

Link Holman was coming back to the boardinghouse, if for no other reason than to get away from his brother Dave and Derek Morrell bickering all the time. He wanted some quiet, but as he approached the house he looked up and saw someone standing in the window.

The window of his room.

He turned and started back the way he had come.

"Shut up!" Link told Dave and Morrell.

They were right on the street corner where he had left them, still arguing like a married couple—complete with the hate.

"Shut the hell up, you two!"

They both stopped and looked at him.

"Hell," Link said, "one of you should just shoot the other and get it over with."

"What the hell is eatin' you?" Dave asked,

"I went back to the house and saw somebody in the window of my room."

"What?" Morrell asked.

"You heard me. It looked like James Earp, and I don't think he was alone."

"What was he doing in your room?" Dave asked.

"I don't know," Link said, "but if he was in mine, I'll bet he was in yours, too."

"I heard somethin' about the Earps bein' crooks," Morrell said, "but I don't have anythin' for them to steal."

"Me, neither."

"Then why would they be in our rooms?" Link wondered. "What are they lookin' for?"

"Maybe they're just curious," Dave said. "Maybe they do that with everybody who stays there."

"Yeah, maybe," Link said, "or maybe you did some-thin' stupid."

"Me? Why me?" Dave demanded.

"Who else has a history of doin' somethin' stupid, Dave?" Link asked.

"Why don't we just go back and ask 'em what they want," Morrell said.

"No," Link said, "we have to go get a drink. It's time I told you boys why we came here. Maybe this is just what we needed."

"Needed for what?" Dave asked.

"Let's go find a place that serves beer and we'll talk about it."

"I heard the Gem serves liquor," Dave said.

"Fine," Link said, "we'll go there."

They went to the Gem Saloon, and because it was after-noon, they easily found a table that gave them some privacy. Link sent Dave to the bar for three beers, and quickly talked to Morrell.

"What's Dave been up to, Derek?" he asked.

"Well, you know as well as I do. He's been seein' that nigger girl who cooks at the boardinghouse."

"And that's it?"

"That's all I know," Morrell said. "He ain't my brother, he's yours."

"Yeah, I know. And what have you been up to since we got here, Derek?"

Before he could answer, Dave came over with the three beers and set them all down without spilling a drop.

"You know what I heard from the bartender?" he asked.

"What?" Link asked.

"There was a murder last night," Dave said. "A young girl at the hotel had her throat cut."

"A young girl?" Link asked.

"Yeah."

"What was her name?" Morrell asked.

"I dunno, but it's supposed to be in the newspaper today."

"Dave, go see if you can get a newspaper from the bartender," Link said.

"Okay," Dave said, picking up his beer, "first just let me—"

"Go now, Dave!"

"Okay!"

Dave put down his beer and went back to the bar. He returned with a copy of the *Colton Chronicle*.

"Gimme that."

Link read the story on the front page. It said that a woman named Sally Quest, who was visiting the city of Colton, had been killed in her room the night before.

"Damn it!"

Link slapped the newspaper down.

"What's wrong?" Dave asked.

Morrell picked up the paper and looked at it.

"She was supposed to pay us to kill Virgil and James Earp," Link said.

"Both of them?"

"Yeah."

"Did you get any money from her up-front?"

"Some," Link said, "but not much."

"Well . . . who killed her?" Dave asked.

"It doesn't say," Morrell said, putting the newspaper down.

"Link, where did you meet this girl?" Dave asked.

"Ouray," Link said, "when we passed through there. She said the Earps killed her father."

"All of them?" Dave asked. "Wyatt, too?"

"She said they all had to die," Link said.

"Well," Dave said, "she's dead now. She ain't payin' us. Let's just get out of town."

"No," Link said.

"Why not?"

"They're lookin' for us," Morrell said. "Besides, there's still the Gunsmith."

"You want to try him, don't you?" Dave asked.

"Don't you?" Morrell asked.

"Not me," Dave said. "I'm no gunman."

"Link?" Morrell asked.

"I'd still like to know who killed the girl," Link said. "She was gonna pay us a lot of money."

THIRTY-FIVE

"They're not comin' back," James said, hours later.

"Their gear is here," Virgil said.

"What gear?" Clint asked. "There's nothing in that room that can't be replaced."

"So you think they figured out we're lookin' for them and left town?" James asked.

"No, I don't think so," Clint said. "If one of them killed that girl, he had a reason."

"Maybe," James said, "he just killed her for her money."

"She was here for a reason," Clint said. "I think she got killed for more of a reason than just her money."

"Then where are they?" James asked. "What are they up to now?"

"That's what Virgil and I are going to find out," Clint said.

"You can go back to your paperwork, little brother," Virgil said. "Clint and I are going back out on the streets."

"I could come with you—"

"No," Virgil said, "this is my job."

"And what am I supposed to do if they do come back here?" James asked.

"They won't," Clint said. "If they do, just stay away from them."

Clint and Virgil left the house and started walking back toward Philadelphia Street.

"What do you think happened?" Virgil asked.

"I think one of them spotted your brother in the window," Clint said.

"That's what I think," Virgil said. "So where are they now?"

"I think," Clint said, "we better assume they're around every corner."

For want of a better place to go, Clint and Virgil returned to the scene of the crime, the Hotel Colton. Virgil grabbed a couple of wooden chairs from the lobby, and they sat down just outside the door.

"Think this is a good idea, puttin' ourselves on display like this?" Virgil asked.

"It's my guess one of these three killed Sally Quest," Clint said. "It's also my guess they want to come after us—or, to be more specific, you."

"Me? Why me?"

"When they came to town, they had no idea I was here," Clint said. "And you're an Earp. And a pretty famous one, to boot."

"Wyatt's the famous one," Virgil said.

"Well, you're more famous than your other brother or your father," Clint said. "I think they came here looking for you."

"Why?"

"I don't know," Clint said, "but it's got something to do with Sally Quest coming here and lying to you."

"What could that young girl have had against me?" Virgil wondered.

"I don't know," Clint said, "and we may never find out."

"Well," Virgil said, "all your guesses could also be wrong."

"True," Clint said, "but do you have any better guesses?"

"At the moment," Virgil said, "no, I don't."

"Then I suggest we just sit here for now."

"Okay," Virgil said, "but bein' on display like this is givin' me an awful itch."

From down the street Link Holman watched as Clint Adams and Virgil Earp sat themselves down in front of the hotel. He backed off then, a few hundred feet down a side street, where his brother Dave and Derek Morrell were waiting.

"What are they doin'?" Dave asked.

"They're just sittin' in front of the hotel," Link said.

"They're just tryin' to draw us out," Morrell said.

"We ain't gonna face 'em on the street, are we?" Dave asked.

"Whatsa matter, boy?" Morrell asked. "Lost your nerve? Oh wait, that's right, you never had any."

"Derek, damn it—"

"Shut up, the both of you," Link said. "Derek, can you take Adams?"

"How the hell do I know if I can take him?" Morrell asked. "But I'm willin' to try."

"Dave, you and me can take Earp."

"That's Wyatt Earp's brother, Link," Dave said.

"I thought that didn't bother you," Link said. "Wasn't that you sayin' how Wyatt Earp had Doc Holliday?"

"Yeah, and you and Derek pointed out we're dealin' with the Gunsmith."

"Derek will deal with the Gunsmith," Link said. "You and me, we're takin' care of Virgil Earp."

"For a dead girl who didn't pay us?" Dave asked. "This is crazy."

"You want out, Dave?" Link asked. "You gonna turn on your own blood?"

"I ain't turnin' on ya, Link," Dave said. "I just think there's gotta be a better way. Why face 'em fair and square?"

"Because that's the only way you get a rep," Morrell said. "And since we're not gettin' paid, we might as well come out of this with a reputation."

"What for?" Dave asked. "What good's a reputation with a gun when we're movin' into a new century, where gunmen are gonna be a thing of the past?"

Morrell got in Dave's face.

"You sayin' I'm a thing of the past, boy?"

"Derek, goddamnit," Dave said, "we're all gonna be a thing of the past soon."

"That's enough, Dave," Link said. "If we're gonna do this, we might as well do it now."

Link started down Philadelphia Street, followed willingly by Derek Morrell, and reluctantly by Dave Holman.

They were walking toward the hotel, when Link

suddenly said, "Wait! Ain't that—" He squinted. "That policeman is walkin' over to them. Quick."

Link stepped into a doorway, leaving both Morrell and Dave to find their own.

THIRTY-SIX

Inspector James crossed the street and approached the hotel.

"Not who I expected to see," Clint said to Virgil as the policeman came up to them.

"What's he want?" Virgil wondered.

"Good evening, gentlemen," the inspector said.

"Inspector," Virgil said. "What brings you here?"

"You two, actually," the inspector said.

"Why is that?" Clint asked.

"I believe you two know more than you're telling me," the policeman said.

"I don't understand, Inspector," Virgil said. "We've cooperated with you all day."

"Yes," James said, "you've been too cooperative."

"We're just sitting here, minding our own business, Inspector," Clint said. "And staying out of your way, as we said we would. What makes you think we're doing anything different?"

"You each have too much of a reputation to just sit

out here, putting yourselves on display, unless you have something up your sleeves."

"I've got nothing up my sleeve," Clint said. "Do you, Virgil?"

"I don't even know what that means," Virgil said. "Is that some Eastern sayin'?"

"Come on, gents," the inspector said, "we can help each other. Tell me why the girl was killed."

"We don't know why she was killed, Inspector," Clint said. "All we know is that she wanted Virgil to find her missing sister."

"She never had a sister," the inspector said.

"Yeah, we found that out, later," Virgil said.

"So then why was she paying you to find one, when she didn't exist?" Inspector James asked.

"We don't have any idea," Virgil said, "and that's the truth."

"Why would we tell you anything but the truth, Inspector?" Clint asked.

"I've been a policeman in many different cities, Mr. Adams," the inspector said. "Would you like to know what I learned along the way?"

"I'd love to know what you learned along the way," Clint said.

"Everybody lies to a policeman," the inspector said. "Even if they don't particularly have anything to hide. It's just something that people do."

"Makes somebody wonder why someone would want to be a policeman," Virgil said.

"Not just policemen," the inspector said. "Lawmen. Come on, you've both worn a badge. Didn't you find people lying to you for no good reason?"

"If I thought someone was lying to me," Virgil said, "I made sure it didn't go on very long."

"I think it was a little different in Dodge and Tombstone than it is here, Mr. Earp," the inspector said. "I don't have your brother Wyatt, or Doc Holliday, to back me up. I do, however, have the two of you."

"You have a whole police department," Clint said.

"Made up of inexperienced young men," the inspector pointed out.

"Hire older men," Clint suggested.

"I'm not in charge of the hiring," James said. "But I am in charge of finding out who killed this young woman, and I need your help."

Clint and Virgil exchanged a glance.

"Yes, I know, I asked you to stay out of it, but I don't believe for a moment that you have done that. So I'm asking you both, what have you found out?"

Clint looked again at Virgil, who shrugged.

"Inspector," Clint said, "why don't you go inside and grab a chair?"

THIRTY-SEVEN

Clint wasn't sure how much he and Virgil were actually going to tell the inspector, but Virgil seemed to leave the decision up to him, so he told the man everything.

"You don't have guests check in when they come to stay at the boardinghouse?" the inspector asked, looking at Virgil.

"First, it's not my boardinghouse, it's my brother's," Virgil said, "so I have nothin' to do with any decisions. Second, it's not a hotel, where guests are required to check in with their full names and addresses. I think all they ever get is a first name—oh, and the money."

"So what names did they get?"

"Link, Dave, and . . ." Virgil said.

"Derek," Clint finished.

"So you believe one of these men killed Sally Quest," Inspector James said.

"Whichever one has the scar on his face," Clint said.

"And you think they came to Colton specifically to come after Mr. Earp here? Why?"

"Either because his name is Earp," Clint said, "or because Sally Quest hired them."

"And why would she do that?" the inspector asked.

"We don't know," Clint said.

"So now you plan to stay out here until the three men come after you?"

"It seems like our best course of action," Clint replied.

"I'm not so sure about that," James said. "We don't really want a shoot-out in the street, do we?"

"Where would you prefer we do it?" Virgil asked. "In a corral? You know, the so called O.K. Corral didn't even take place in a—"

"What Virgil's trying to say is," Clint said, cutting his friend off, "we'll try to do it as safely as possible, but that's pretty much going to be up to the three men. If we leave the place to them, though, they might just decide to do it in a crowd."

"I can send some men over—"

"Not a good idea," Clint said.

"Why not?"

"If they see your men, they might just give it up and leave town. You'll never get your killer that way."

James shifted uncomfortably in his chair.

"Tell me again," he said, "why they don't just leave town now?"

Virgil finally joined in, and between him and Clint they convinced Inspector James not to bring in a dozen of his men to back them up.

"I don't know about this," James still said, shaking his head.

"This is the way we do things out here, Inspector," Virgil told him. "We handle them ourselves."

"You don't have a badge on, Mr. Earp," James said. "It will be very difficult for me to explain this to my chief."

"So wait until it's all over," Virgil said, "and then let me explain it to him. I'm used to having to justify my own decisions."

"I have my pistol on me," the inspector said. "I could stay and—"

"They won't try anything if you stay here, Inspector," Clint said. "There has to be no badges around. They don't mind witnesses, but no badges."

"That's true," Virgil said.

"Why witnesses?"

"That's what they'll want," Clint said, "witnesses to the fact that they killed Virgil Earp . . ."

"Not to mention the Gunsmith," Virgil finished.

Reluctantly the inspector stood up.

"I am only agreeing to this because I want this killer," he said. "The way that girl was cut up . . . well, it was a damn shame."

"We're agreed on that," Clint said.

"Do you have any idea how long this will take?" the inspector asked.

"My guess is they won't want to leave it too long," Clint said. "They'll want to get it done and then get out of town."

"So . . . tonight?"

"That would be quick," Virgil said. "If they're watching us, they've seen you come over to us. Now they'll want to be sure there are no policemen around when they do come after us."

"My best guess would be tomorrow," Clint said. "They'll probably leave us sitting here tonight, thinking we might become . . . antsy."

"Nervous?" the inspector asked.

"No, Inspector," Virgil said, "I don't think they think we'll get nervous."

"No, no," the inspector said, "of course not. Er, sorry. I'm sure you've been through this so many times before it's become second nature."

Clint and Virgil exchanged a glance, decided not to comment on the statement. If the inspector thought it was easy for them to kill another human being, let him.

"I'm not sure I'm doing the right thing here," the inspector said.

"None of us will know that for sure until later," Clint said, "and maybe not even then."

THIRTY-EIGHT

Link Holman watched the inspector walk away from Clint Adams and Virgil Earp, then signaled his brother and Derek Morrell to back up. They got off Philadelphia Street and onto a side street.

"Now what?" Morrell asked.

"Not today."

"What? But we're all ready."

"Yeah, and so are they," Link said.

"What makes you say that?" Dave asked.

"Well, look at them," Link said. "They're just sittin' there. They're waitin' for us."

"But do they know it's us they're waitin' for?" Morrell asked.

"What may be more important," Link said, "is did they tell that policeman about us?"

"Jesus," Dave said, "if they did, and he comes back with a bunch of men—"

"You think he's gonna try to arrest us?" Morrell asked.

Link hesitated before answering.

"You saw them sittin' there together, right? I think Adams and Earp talked the police into lettin' them handle everythin'."

"So then he ain't comin' back with more men," Dave said. " 'Cause if he is, we gotta get outta town, Link."

"No," Link said, "I think as far as the police go, we're okay."

"And what about Adams and Earp?" Morrell asked.

"I think they wanna handle it the way they would have in Dodge or Tombstone or Wichita," Link said, "and not the way it would be handled in a new, growing city like Colton."

"In the street?" Morrell asked.

"With guns," Link said. "I don't know about the street, but with guns."

"We can do that," Morrell said.

"Yeah, but not today," Link said. "We're gonna make them wait."

"So where do we spend the night?" Dave asked.

"We split up and find a place," Link said. "Then we get back together in the mornin'."

"Where?" Morrell asked.

"That's what we're gonna decide," Link said, "but let's get away from here."

As the inspector walked away, Virgil said, "That went better than I expected."

"Me, too," Clint said. "I didn't think he'd just walk away."

"Guess we'll have to see if he stays away," Virgil said. "Ya know, we just had a pretty public meetin' with a member of the police department."

"I know where you're going," Clint said. "This isn't going to work, now. They're not going to come walking right up to us."

"We're gonna have to find them," Virgil said. "Only they won't be comin' back to the boardinghouse, so where do we look?"

"How many employees does your brother have besides Kate?"

"Kate's not an employee, she's a partner."

"Oh, right."

"Don't make that mistake in front of her," Virgil warned him.

"I won't. Anyway, I think they have a girl who cleans and then they have another one—Regina—who cooks."

"We should talk to them, see if they saw or heard anything about these men."

"Okay," Virgil said. "Kate or James can tell us where to find them. We can take one each."

"Virgil," Clint said, "maybe we should stick together. We don't want anything to happen like it did back in Tombstone."

Virgil looked down at his crippled arm.

"I appreciate the thought behind that, Clint, but I can still take care of myself," he said.

"I know that," Clint said, "I just thought we'd both be safer from ambush if we stuck together."

Virgil thought a moment, then said, "Okay, then. Let's get back to the boardinghouse . . . together."

Inspector James walked away from his "meeting" with Clint Adams and Virgil Earp with second thoughts. If he let this turn into another O.K. Corral, he was going to have a lot of explaining to do to his boss.

He had two or three men he counted heavily on, men he could trust. He was going to have to have a meeting with them as soon as possible.

THIRTY-NINE

Inspector James stared at the three men he'd called into his office.

"You three are the only men in this department I trust implicitly."

"Huh?" one of them said.

"I trust you," James said. "To do what you're supposed to do."

"Yessir."

"Do any of you know Virgil Earp?"

"Yes, sir," one said.

"Sir," a second one chimed in.

"Good," James said. "He is sitting in front of the Hotel Colton with another man. That man is Clint Adams."

"The Gunsmith?" one of them asked, eyes wide.

"That's right," James said. "I want the three of you to get over there, watch them, and don't let them see you. Understand?"

"Yes, sir," one said.

"What are we watching for, sir?" another asked.

"Trouble," James said. "I'm expecting three men to

try to kill them. I don't want Virgil Earp or the Gunsmith to get killed in Colton. We would never live it down."

"Yes, sir."

"And don't wear your uniforms," James said. "Get changed, and get over there as soon as you can."

"Yes, sir."

"Anything that doesn't look right, one of you come back and report to me."

"Yes, sir."

"Now go!"

The three men changed from their uniforms and hurried over to the Hotel Colton. When they got there, they saw three chairs in front of the hotel, but nobody was sitting in them.

"This don't look right," the first of them said.

"Better get back to headquarters and tell the inspector," the second said. "We'll stay here. Maybe they'll come back."

"And maybe it's all over," the third man said.

They all looked at one another and had the same thought. Hopefully, they wouldn't get blamed for anything.

When James saw Kate lead Clint and Virgil into his office, he sat back.

"Come to rescue me again?"

"New plan," Clint said. "We need to talk to the women who work for you."

"Regina and Alice?"

"I know where Regina lives," Kate said to James, "but you hired Alice recently."

"Regina just cooks, and Alice cleans," James said. "What can they know?"

"That's what we want to find out," Virgil said.

"Well, okay." James shuffled some papers, then wrote down an address and handed it to Virgil. "Alice is just a kid. She lives with her parents. She comes in twice a week, has almost no contact with our guests."

"Has she been in since your three guests came?" Clint asked.

"No."

Clint looked at Virgil, who said, "It may not make any sense to talk with her, but Regina . . ."

"Yes, she's cooked breakfast for them," Kate said, "talked to them. Heard them talking amongst themselves. She might know something."

"Who does she live with?" Clint asked.

"She has five kids."

"No man?" Clint asked.

"No."

"What's her address?"

"I don't know," she said, "but I can take you there."

"Let's go, then," Clint said.

"James?" she said.

"I'll stay here," James said. "You go."

"Okay," Virgil said to Kate. "Lead the way."

As they approached the small house Regina lived in with her family, they saw five small figures sitting on the front step. As they got closer, Clint could see that these were her children. They were all apparently girls, although the older girl seemed to be holding an infant in her arms.

They walked up to the children, who all stared up at them with wide eyes.

"Melissa," Kate said to the older girl, who appeared to be about eleven or twelve, "where's your mama?"

"She's inside."

"What is she doin'?"

The girl shrugged.

"Why are you out here with your sisters?"

"Mama has a visitor," she said. "She don't like us to be inside when she got a visitor."

Clint looked at Virgil.

"You think?" he asked.

"Could be."

"Kate," Clint said, "take all the children across the way,"

"To where?" she asked.

"Just away from the house."

"All right, girls," Kate said, "come with me." She herded the children across the street and away from the house. Clint and Virgil both drew their guns.

"I'll go around to the back," Clint said. "See if you can get the front door open."

Virgil nodded. Clint moved around to the side of the house, but before he could get to the back he looked in a window and stopped. There was a black woman on a bed, naked, on her belly, her face pushed down into her pillow. The white man straddling her was driving his penis in and out of her from behind. Clint was surprised the woman was quiet, but that was probably for the benefit of her kids. He wondered, though, why she wasn't suffocating with her face in the pillow like that.

At that moment all three of them heard something from the front of the house. Apparently, the flimsy shack had a good front door, and Virgil had been unable to force it without making some kind of noise.

The man's head jerked around. Clint saw his face. But did not recognize him.

Through the window Clint heard the woman say, "Who dat? Dat my kids?"

The man didn't answer. He got off the bed and grabbed his gun, moved toward the bedroom door, which was also closed. If Virgil came through that door, he'd be dead before he knew it.

Clint smashed out the window, pointed his gun into the room, and said, "Hold it!"

The naked man turned his head toward the window, then brought the gun around. At that moment the bedroom door crashed open. The black girl had screamed at the sound of breaking glass, and she screamed again when the door slammed open.

Clint fired once. The bullet hit the man in the chest, driving him backward until the back of his legs hit the bed. He fell over on top of the girl, who kept right on screaming.

FORTY

"She says he never forced himself on her," Virgil told Clint later. "Says she wanted him to come to her house with her. She says he was nice to her."

They had taken Regina from the bedroom—after letting her get dressed—and put her in the other room with her kids. Kate stayed there with her. Clint and Virgil were in the bedroom with the body.

"She say his name?" Clint asked.

Virgil nodded.

"She says his name was Dave."

"Okay, so he's one of the guests at the boarding-house," Clint said. "Where are the other two?"

"And why did they split up?" Virgil asked. Then he looked at Clint. "Makes them harder to find."

"Maybe the other two," Clint said. "Turns out this one was easy to find."

"What about the law?" Virgil asked.

Clint studied the body.

"No," Clint said. "Let's keep this quiet for now."

"What does that get us?"

"Tomorrow morning there'll be two men wondering where this one went."

"So what do we do with the body?"

"Well, let's get it out of here so these kids don't have a body in their home. We can take it out the back door."

"And take it where?"

"You tell me, you live here," Clint said. "Where's a good place to stash a body for a while?"

"Probably an abandoned barn."

"You got one in mind?"

"Yeah, not too far from here, but we'll need a horse, or a buckboard."

"Buckboard," Clint said. "A body tied to the back of a horse is too noticeable. We can hide it better in a buckboard."

"Okay, then," Virgil said, "first we need a buckboard. I know where to get one."

"Pull it up to the back of the house," Clint said. "We'll wrap the body in this sheet. It's all bloody anyway."

"Right," Virgil said. "I'll meet you in the back."

Virgil left to get a buckboard, and Clint went into the other room, where the women and the children were.

"Is he dead?" Regina asked.

"Yes."

"Why?" she asked. "He waren't rapin' me, mister. I axed him to come here."

"He and his friends are outlaws, Regina," Clint said. "We wanted to talk to him, but he grabbed his gun. I didn't have a choice."

"What's rapin'?" one of her daughters asked.

"Hesh up!" Regina said.

"Actually, we came here to talk to you."

"To me? What about?"

"About them. We wanted to know what you heard them talking about, if anything."

"Dey didn't talk in fron' of me," she said. "Dave's the only one talked ta me."

"What did he say?"

"You know," she said, "things ta get me into bed."

"Whose bed, Mama?" another daughter asked.

"I said hesh!"

"You tol' Lulu Belle to hesh, not me."

"Well, now I wants you all to hesh."

"Did Dave tell you what he and his friends were doing in Colton, Regina?"

"He tol' me one of dem other mens was his brother," she said. "He tol' me de other one was a gunfighter."

"Derek? Or Link?"

"Link is de brother."

"And he never told you why they were here?"

"No. He jes' come here to be wit' me."

"Did he . . . pay you to let him come here?" Kate asked.

"No," she said. "I ain't no whore, Miss Kate."

"I know that, Regina," Kate said. "I'm sorry."

"What we gon' do now?" Regina asked. "Is I gon' be arrested?"

"No, no," Clint said. "We're going to take the body away and you won't have to worry about this, Regina. I promise."

Regina looked at Kate.

"You can trust Mr. Adams, Regina," she said. "And Mr. Earp. They'll take care of everything."

Regina, sitting with her kids gathered around her, looked up at Clint and said, "I thanks you, Mr. Adams."

"That's okay, Regina," Clint said, "I'm sorry this had to happen." He looked at Kate. "You wait here with her. I'll go and wait for Virgil. When he gets here, we'll take the body away."

"All right," Kate said. "I'll just wait here until you're done."

Clint nodded, then went outside to wait for Virgil.

FORTY-ONE

Clint was waiting out back when Virgil pulled up in the buckboard. Together they went inside, rolled the body up in the sheet, and transferred it to the buckboard. Clint went back in to talk to Kate.

"Why don't you help Regina clean up, and then we'll see you back at the house."

"Okay, Clint," she said. "Come on, Regina, let's feed your kids, and then clean up."

Clint left them to it. He went outside and climbed up onto the buckboard with Virgil.

Link Holman and Derek Morrell had not yet split up when they spotted Virgil Earp driving down the street in a buckboard.

"What's he up to?" Morrell wondered aloud.

"I don't know," Link said. "Why don't we find out?"

It wasn't hard for them to follow the buckboard on foot, because it wasn't going very fast. When it pulled to a stop behind a house, Link and Morrell found some cover to watch from.

"Ain't this that nigger gal's house?" Morrell asked.

"Yeah," Link said. "Dave was gonna come here and spend the night."

As they watched, Clint Adams and Virgil Earp carried something wrapped in a bloody sheet out to the buckboard.

"Ah, Christ," Link said.

"You thinkin' that's Dave?" Morrell asked.

"Yeah," Link said. "They got him, Derek. They killed Dave."

Clint and Virgil drove the buckboard away.

"You wanna follow them and see where they take 'im?" Morrell asked.

"No," Link said, "I got a better idea. Come on."

Virgil had found an abandoned barn where they could stash the body. He and Clint unloaded it and then got back on the buckboard.

"You rent this?" Clint asked.

"No, I borrowed it from somebody who can keep his mouth shut."

"Who's that?"

"Nick. I gotta bring it back."

"I'll come with you, and then we can go back to the boardinghouse."

"And do what?" Virgil snapped the reins at the horse to get it going.

"Figure out our next move, I guess," Clint said. "We got one of them. Now we've got to get the other two."

"Well, I hope it don't take too long," Virgil said. "We're gonna have to explain to the inspector why we hid this body."

"Once we give him his killer, he won't care," Clint said.

"I hope you're right."

They took the buckboard back to Nick, unhitched the horse for him, even cleaned some blood off the flatbed before they left.

It was getting dark when they walked back to the rooming house, entered, and were immediately attacked by Kate.

"James is gone!" she said.

"So he went home," Virgil said. "Allie probably made di—"

"No, no," she said. "His office is a shambles, like there was a fight."

Virgil rushed past her, followed by Clint. Kate brought up the rear.

As she had said, the office was a mess. On the floor, amid a mess of paperwork, was James's gun.

"They took him," Virgil said.

"They must know about Dave," Clint said.

"How could they?" Kate asked.

"Maybe they saw us moving the body," Clint said.

"So we killed his brother, the one named Link, and now Link's got James," Virgil said. "An eye for an eye."

"You have to get him back," Kate said. "What are you gonna tell Allie?"

"I don't know," Virgil said.

"You're lucky you weren't here when they came, Kate," Clint said, "or they'd have you."

"I'm not looking to lose a partner, Clint," she said. "You have to get him back."

"I'm not gonna lose another brother," Virgil said.

"Don't worry, Kate," Clint said. "We'll get him back." Clint took hold of Virgil's good shoulder. "We'll get him back, Virgil."

FORTY-TWO

Virgil stared out the front window.

"We can't just wait," he said.

"What else can we do?" Clint asked. "Where is there to look? We've got to wait to hear from them."

"What makes you think they won't just kill him?" Virgil asked.

"Let's turn it around," Clint said. "What if they had killed James first, and then you grabbed Dave? What would you want to do?"

"Kill him in front of his brother," Virgil said. "I see."

Kate came in carrying a tray with mugs of coffee on it.

"I know you're not hungry, but I made coffee."

Clint stared down at the black liquid in the cups.

"You made it?"

"Taste it before you turn your nose up at it," she said.

Actually, it didn't smell too bad. It smelled strong, the way he liked it.

He picked up one mug, Virgil a second. The third remained on the tray.

Clint sipped.

"Well?" Kate asked.

"Not bad," he said. Strong, like it smelled.

"That's a relief," she said. "Now I'll have some."

"I wouldn't," Virgil said. "It'll melt your teeth."

"I thought coffee was supposed to be strong," she said.

"It is," Clint said.

"You two deserve each other," Virgil said, putting the mug down. He went back to looking out the window.

Kate sipped the coffee.

"Is this the way it's supposed to taste?" she asked Clint.

"It's close enough."

They both looked at Virgil.

"I searched James's office, just in case there was a note in among the papers. There wasn't."

"They'll send someone in the morning with a message," Clint said.

"Send who?" Virgil asked. "Who else do they know in Colton?"

"They'll probably grab a kid and send him," Clint said. "Maybe the hotel clerk."

"You know they're gonna kill James, and try to kill us," Virgil said.

"I know they're gonna try to kill all three of us."

"You don't have to come with me."

"Yes," Clint said, "I do."

"We'll need backup guns."

"Mine's in the hotel."

"Mine's in my office," Virgil said, "and I've got one at home."

"You can take James's," Clint said.

"What about you?"

"If I have a chance, I'll stop by the hotel," Clint said. "If not, I'll have to do without."

Virgil looked at Clint.

"If there's a shot to be taken, I want you to take it," he said. "You're the best shot I've ever seen with a handgun."

"Okay, Virgil."

"I'm gonna trust you with my brother's life."

"If I take the shot," Clint said, "I'll make it."

"How do you know?" Kate asked.

"What?"

"How do you know you'll make the shot? How do you know you won't miss?"

"With James's life hanging in the balance," Clint said, "missing is not an option."

"It must be nice to be that confident."

"Confidence has nothing to do with it," Clint said. "If I miss, I'll have to explain it to Virgil, to Allie, and to Wyatt. And to you. Missing is not in the equation."

"What if they make you drop your guns?"

"That's not an option, either," Virgil said. "If we drop our weapons, we're all dead."

"So there has to be a shooting?"

"Can't be avoided," Clint said. "Just like in Tombstone."

"I wasn't in Tombstone," she said. "I don't know if that couldn't have been avoided. But this—why not go to the police?"

"The police," Virgil said, "would definitely get James killed. No, this has to be done by me and Clint. There's no way around it."

"Trust us," Clint said. "We know what has to be done here."

Kate shook her head and said, "Men."

FORTY-THREE

"Clint!"

Clint came to on the sofa and stared up at Virgil, who hadn't slept all night.

"I'm up," he said. "Sorry."

"That's okay," Virgil said. "One of us had to sleep. I'm happy it was you. Your eyes will be clear."

At that point there was a knock at the door.

"I'll get it," Virgil said, glancing out the window to see who it was as he headed to the door.

Kate came out of the kitchen with coffee while Virgil went to the door.

"I thought you could use this," she said, handing Clint a mug. "I made it even stronger."

He sipped it and nodded.

"Yes, you did."

Virgil came in.

"Let's go," he said. "That was the messenger."

"Messenger?" Kate asked.

"Like Clint said, a boy, about ten."

"Did he bring a note?"

"No," Virgil said, "he's gonna take us to the meeting place."

"Why wouldn't they send a note?" Kate asked.

"Because then we'd have time to find the place," Clint said.

Virgil picked up James's gun and stuck it in the back of his belt.

"We have to go now," Virgil said. "No time to stop at the hotel."

"Wait!" Kate said.

She ran from the room, and returned in a moment carrying a gun.

"What is that?" Virgil asked,

"It's my gun," she said. "Clint's backup gun."

Clint looked at it. It was a .25-caliber Colt New Line, similar to the one in his room.

"That's not a gun."

"It's a gun," Clint said, taking it from Kate. "Thanks, Kate." He stuck it in the back of his belt, turned to Virgil. "Let's go."

Link Holman checked the ropes that bound James Earp's hands behind his back.

"Remember, Derek," he said. "I get Earp, you take the Gunsmith."

"I got it, Link," Morrell said. "You've only told me ten times."

Link turned and slammed both hands into Morrell's chest.

"Just don't miss!"

"Too bad we can't both hide behind an Earp," Morrell said.

"What's that supposed to mean?"

"I think you know what it means, Link," Morrell said. "This is supposed to be done man-to-man, face-to-face. Two of us, two of them. You're gonna hide behind Earp's brother."

"I'm gonna make sure I avenge my brother's death," Link said.

"The idiot," Morrell said. "He's dead because he had to be with that nigger bitch."

"You're gonna do this, Derek," Link said, "and if you have a problem with me, we'll deal with it after."

"I should walk away and let you handle this yourself," Morrell said, "but I won't."

Link grabbed Morrell's arm and squeezed it. "Okay, Derek."

"Do you two want to be alone?" James Earp asked.

"This is as far as I go," the boy said. His name was Tom and he was eleven, not ten.

"What?" Virgil asked.

"Where do we go, Tom?" Clint asked.

"Around that corner," the boy said. "The man said they'd be in a corral."

"In a what?" Virgil asked.

"A corral."

Tom turned and ran back the way they had come.

Virgil looked at Clint.

"They gotta be kiddin'," he said.

"Virgil," Clint said, "you've got to take care of the man who's not standing behind James."

"What makes you think either of them will be standing behind him?"

"They took him, they're going to use him," Clint said. "Just remember. The one out in the open is yours."

"I'll remember," Virgil said. "You just remember what you said about not missing."

"Not an option," Clint said.

FORTY-FOUR

As they turned the corner, they saw three men standing in a corral next to an abandoned barn. One of them was standing behind James Earp, who seemed to have his hands tied behind him.

"That's it," one of them said. "Come a little closer."

Clint and Virgil moved closer.

"Come on, Earp," the man standing behind James said. "Your family likes corrals. Come on in."

Clint unhitched the gate and swung it open. But instead of stepping in, he and Virgil stopped there.

"This is far enough," Clint said.

"That ain't for you to say, Adams," the man said. "That's for Earp."

"What's your name?" Virgil asked.

"I'm Link Holman," the man said. "You killed my brother, Dave."

Virgil didn't bother to tell the man that it was Clint who'd killed his brother. In the scheme of things it didn't matter.

"And now I've got your brother," Link said.

"And who's your friend?" Clint asked. "We might as well all get acquainted."

"This is Derek Morrell, Adams," Link said. "The man who's gonna kill you."

"So I guess that means you're gonna kill me," Virgil said.

"I mean to," Link said. "You gents just toss your guns away now."

"What kind of shoot-out would this be if we tossed away our guns?" Clint asked.

"The kind where you two die," Link said. "If ya don't wanna toss them away, you get to watch Mr. James Earp here die."

Link Holman was only slightly bigger than James. He wasn't giving Clint much of a shot, using James to hide behind the way he was—but there was a shot. Link had to move his head to the side a bit so he could see Clint and Morrell. That gave Clint his right eye as a target.

"We tossin'?" Virgil asked Clint.

"Let's not bother with it," Clint said. "Let's just get this done."

"You got a shot?"

"I got one."

"Damned if I see it," Virgil said.

"What's it gonna be?" Link Holman shouted.

"I think we should stop talking and get this done," Clint called back.

"You stupid—" Link Holman started, but Clint simply drew and fired, hoping that Virgil would handle Derek Morrell.

* * *

James Earp heard Clint's shot go by him, then felt something wet on his neck. Damn it, Clint Adams, he thought, you shot me!

Virgil drew when Clint did and fired one shot at Derek Morrell. Morrell got his gun out, but never brought it to bear, as Virgil's shot hit him in the chest. The man fell over backward, his gun flying from his hand.

James turned quickly, his hand going to his neck. He looked at the blood that stained his palm and realized it wasn't his. He then looked down at Link Holman, who was missing his right eye.

Clint and Virgil walked up to James.

"You okay, little brother?" Virgil asked.

"Jesus," James said to Clint, "how'd you make that shot?"

"There was no other option," Clint said.

Virgil slapped Clint on the back and said, "Thank you."

When Clint and Virgil got to the police station, there was a ruckus going on. Townspeople were outside, and uniformed police were keeping them at bay. There was also a reporter from the local paper.

"What's going on?" Clint asked.

"They caught the guy who killed that Quest woman," the reporter said.

"Is that a fact?" Virgil asked.

"Who was it?" Clint asked.

"The desk clerk at the Hotel Colton," the man said. "From what I hear he tried to force himself on the girl, then cut her throat when she tried to scream."

"Are they sure?" Virgil asked.

"Oh, they're sure," the reporter said. "Inspector James went to the hotel with three of his men for some reason, and I guess the clerk thought they were comin' for him. He confessed."

"Confessed?"

"Yup."

Clint and Virgil backed off a bit, away from the commotion.

"Think this is the time to tell Inspector James he's got three more bodies?" Virgil asked Clint.

"This," Clint said, "is most certainly not the time."

Virgil shrugged and said, "Okay, we'll tell him tomorrow."

Watch for

MESSAGE ON THE WIND

334th novel in the exciting GUNSMITH series
from Jove

Coming in October!

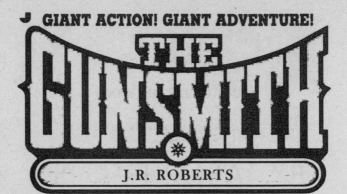

GIANT ACTION! GIANT ADVENTURE!

THE GUNSMITH

J.R. ROBERTS

Little Sureshot And
The Wild West Show
(Gunsmith Giant #9)

Dead Weight
(Gunsmith Giant #10)

Red Mountain
(Gunsmith Giant #11)

The Knights of Misery
(Gunsmith Giant #12)

The Marshal from Paris
(Gunsmith Giant #13)

Lincoln's Revenge
(Gunsmith Giant #14)

penguin.com/actionwesterns

M455AS0509

GIANT-SIZED ADVENTURE FROM AVENGING ANGEL LONGARM.

BY TABOR EVANS

2006 Giant Edition:

LONGARM AND THE OUTLAW EMPRESS

2007 Giant Edition:

LONGARM AND THE GOLDEN EAGLE SHOOT-OUT

2008 Giant Edition:

LONGARM AND THE VALLEY OF SKULLS

2009 Giant Edition:

LONGARM AND THE LONE STAR TRACKDOWN

penguin.com/actionwesterns